Thieves at Heart

The Valley of Ten Crescents Book One

TRISTAN J. TARWATER

To Eliza,

Have a great time at GGC'12!

Make great adventures!

Tristan J Tarwater

Book Design: Christopher Tarwater
Cover Artist: Amy Clare Learmonth
Editor: Annetta Ribken

ISBN:098400890X
ISBN-13:9780984008902

To Christopher

ACKNOWLEDGMENTS

It would be downright terrible of me to not acknowledge some of the amazing people who helped Thieves at Heart and The Valley of Ten Crescents get rolling.

First of all to my spouse and Admin, **Chris**. You put me in the situation where I came up with Tavi, Derk and all the other things in these stories. You put up with me rambling about histories and geographies and religions and topographies. You made the site, learned how to format e-books, web design…and you've supported my writing. I could write a book about how wonderful you are, basically.

SOPI. You can't read yet but if it weren't for you destroying a vast majority of my free time with your fiery personality I wouldn't have turned into a maniac, writing during the scant moments I had. A lot of this was written when you were asleep at night or taking a nap or (finally) playing quietly by yourself. In addition, I wanted to do the thing I most wanted to do so when you get older you feel like you can do the same. Do what you love.

Nathan. My first fan. *fistbump* You read the whole thing. All of it. And talked to me about it. It helped me want to finish the next bit, knowing you were waiting to find out what happened to Tavera. You helped get this all out. Thank you for waiting for all this and always being there for fantasy fun.

Vas! You're such an inspiration and helped me out so much with your encouragement (and provided comics I could veg with when I needed a break). You're my unofficial mentor on how to be professional while still being myself. You are an amazing creator and an amazing person.

Lynn. Thank you for telling me that the story could be better. I really appreciate your honesty. Seriously. And thank you for introducing me to Annetta. You are a great ambassador and representative for the world of self-publishing. And thank you for introducing me to a genre of book I don't normally read!

Annetta, you make editing a total joy. You worked with our deadline and are totally awesome to work with. I honestly was not expecting to get an editor AND a friend but I did. Half this book would not be here if not for you. Literally. You rocked the Valley.

And to all our Lvl 4 Kickstarter Backers: **Jeron Richardson, Brittany McGuire, H. David** and **Nereida Brooks** and **Andrew W. Williams Jr.** Thank you so much for backing this elf up. We really appreciate it.

Chapter 1
Out of the Dregs

"Tavi, I really wish you weighed more, girl. You can never pull these things tight enough!" Prisca the Tart stood up from the bed, examining the ties of the wide belt she wore under her bust in the full length mirror. A look of disappointment came over the woman's highly painted face as she looked over the leather cords crisscrossing her back, brown threaded through pale pink matching the dress she was wearing. Her light eyes lit upon the tiny bit of the girl reflected in the mirror, a small brown hand crawling away once it was noticed. The woman sighed and laughed, brushing out her skirts as she walked back to the bed and sat in front of the little girl, the hay and feathers settling with a rustle under her weight. "Come now, sweets, use those tiny fingers of yours and fix what you've done."

"Yes, mam," came the quiet voice, the girl's head bowed as she went to work. Skinny legs shifted under the girl's small frame and she scratched at her greasy dark hair, what remained of her locks barely long enough to cover one slightly pointed ear. Her hand brushed against the other ear as her hands went to Prisca's laces. Where there was supposed to be a point was instead a straight line, pink and tender where a knife had cut the cartilage away. It still sent a shiver through Tavi when she touched it. The loss of her hair meant she couldn't hide the telltale signs of her blood or her past and her face grew hot even now, recalling Prisca's announcement and remedy. Lice and a shave. "Can't have bugs hopping about when I'm on business," Prisca had said as she shaved off the girl's knotty black locks. Dark eyes glanced towards the mirror and Tavi wondered if she could look at her own reflection without crying yet. The assurance that she wasn't the only girl on the Row to have her head shaved didn't help. Slender, nimble fingers tugged at the cords already warm from the woman's body heat, and the little girl coughed slightly as she worked, pulling back on the ties as hard as she could.

"You're not coming down with something now, are you?" Prisca asked, breathing in sharply as the little girl found a very loose spot and tugged hard. "The minute you start feeling ill, you must let me know so I can get you something for it. Can't have sickness about, you know."

"Just clearing my throat, mam," Tavi said, untying the tie at the top and placing her tiny foot on the woman's ample backside, leaning back with all of her weight and grunting as she did so, the woman holding onto the bed frame so hard her knuckles were white. The girl frowned with a mouth slightly too big for her face and she carefully tied a bow, making sure the cords were the same length at the ends. "I still don't understand why I have to do this if you're to take it off anyway."

"Oh, Tavi dear." Satisfied with the tautness of the garment, the woman turned to look in the mirror again, tucking a blonde curl behind one ear while letting another fall across her face. "You're a bit young to understand, but I'll teach you in time. I don't know how you elfy ones grow, but I suspect sooner than later you'll be ready to answer calls, with the Priestess' blessing." Prisca dipped a finger into a pot of ground clay and vegetable juice, running the digit over her eyelids. The faint smoky color made her blue eyes seem even bluer in the light of the lantern. Tavi watched with some interest as Prisca picked a heartberry out of a bowl of fruit sitting on her nightstand, rubbing it against her teeth and lips before she ate the berry whole. "And," the woman added, holding the fruit out towards Tavi. The little girl pressed her lips together before her dark fingers darted out, picking out a tart greenberry, her face screwing up as its sourness danced across her tongue. Prisca laughed, a sound like a cackle and a chuckle all in one. "You really must start eating more and eating the things I tell you. You're far too thin! Can't have men thinking they'll snap you in two. Your Red Earth will never come if you don't fill out, love."

A bell above the door chimed, the dented metal causing it to ring strangely. Prisca clapped her hands with glee, reaching over for a vial of scented oil she had been gifted recently. The fragrance was of something Tavi had smelled before but couldn't place. Prisca said it was distilled moonflower and something the girl had never heard of that was supposed to 'tighten mens' trousers'. The woman turned the bottle over on her finger and dabbed between her breasts before running the still shining finger across her neck, the way someone might do to indicate they were going to slit someone's throat. She then placed the bottle back on the nightstand, as it had been a gift from the person she was expecting. Prisca had told Tavi it was good to display gifts the customers had given when they visited. Excitement made the woman bounce up and down on the mattress, her hands clasped over her heart. "This could be it!" Prisca squeaked lustily, blushing through her makeup. "I think it is. Make yourself scarce now and have at it, you know what to do." Before the Tart had finished giving her orders, the little girl had already ducked into the space between the walls as always, careful to place the upholstered chair close enough to the secret hiding place so she could reach it easily but still remain hidden as she went about her side of the business.

When she originally started picking the pockets of customers for Prisca the Tart, the anticipation always filled her with fear and excitement. After a few months of sliding back the hidden panel and rummaging around for coins, charms or other things the men would never report stolen to the local brown cloaks it became mundane, almost easy. However, today was different. Tonight was the New Moon, and as Prisca the Tart had always done on the New Moon, she and Brass Sera and Kind Gia went down to the soothsayer to have their fortunes told. The soothsayer was a short, wizened woman, shrouded in a brown, thick cloak. She sat on a street corner, offering fortunes for coin or food. All that was exposed of the woman was her deeply creased face and her curled, spotted hands, gnarled from the twisting sickness some old people got. It made Tavi's skin crawl to look at it. The old woman scared Tavi and she told Prisca as much but her mam had shook her head and laughed in response. The old woman turned the cards over for Prisca and informed her that from a secret place, a boon would be in her room before the moon set.

Tavi could make out her benefactor from behind the false wall, seeing her large bosom rise and fall with each breath. She couldn't let her mam down. Her stomach fluttered as she considered what good fortune would come their way. What would the men have in their pockets? Maybe someone with a good deal of money would take Prisca 'into his pocket' and by association, Tavi would benefit as well. Her mouth felt dry and she licked her lips, waiting, her heart pounding as the sound of booted footsteps came closer.

The door opened and for a few breaths, no one walked in. Then Prisca clapped her hands joyfully and the man entered, closing the door behind him with a low thud shaking the walls. Tavi narrowed her eyes as she looked through the peek-hole. She thought she recognized the boots and strained her ear to listen to what the grown ups were saying.

"Ah, Prisca...beautiful as always," came the deep voice, muffled slightly by distance and wood. His boots were well worn but had once been fine, a deep mahogany brown color offset with tarnished, metal buckles. There was something funny about the heels of the boots and the sound they made whenever he walked in, but the girl could never quite place her fin-ger on it. Prisca stood up from the bed, only to stop short, laughing raucously as the man rushed towards her and threw her down onto the already rumpled sheets and well used mattress.

This was the part Tavi was interested in, though not for the reason most people would be. The little girl silently thanked the goddess that the man had come to collect, and quickly. Sometimes Prisca and her clients would talk for a while, the Tart pouring them a glass of beer or allowing them to read things they had written for her. The more time they spent doing this the longer Tavi had to sit in the crawl space, waiting for an opportune time to get to work. On one occasion a fellow had talked to her mam for so long, Tavi's legs had fallen asleep. Prisca had to pry her out of the wall, laughing the whole time and apologizing while all Tavi could do was cry as the blood rushed back into her legs, drawing tears from her eyes and curses from her young mouth. But the man whose boots she liked and wondered at was making good and quick on his money. She held her breath and listened to be sure that they were fully occupied with one another, the bed creaking and rustling with their movement before the little girl slid back the tiny panel in the wall.

Tavi examined the jacket tossed carelessly onto the high backed chair, the upholstery worn and faded after various types of use. The jacket was unremarkable. The pockets faced her, which would make her job even easier. Depending on whether the event was 'quick and painless,' as her mam told her most business transactions were, or 'pleasure and leisure,' Tavi would decide if she should check for inner pockets, where most of the better items were hidden.

Her hand was wrist deep in the left hand pocket when she heard Prisca squeal and the man say something, the woman laughing in response. Tavi smiled

to herself, a small, excited smile within the dark between the walls. A deeper inspection would be made.

The little girl took a deep breath before creeping
her hand forward, sliding it over the fabric and
through the folds, searching for an inner pocket. A lip
of fabric brushed against her fingertips and she
grinned, listening carefully before letting her fingers
slip into the surprisingly silky soft lining and into the
hidden pocket. Tavi felt something cold and hard, her
tongue slipping its way past her lips as she wondered
what it could be, her fingers trailing over the length of
the object…a dagger?

Before her question could be answered and before she even realized what was happening, there was
a loud thump and the shock of her wrist being
grabbed firmly by a strong hand. She squeaked and
tried to pull her hand back, horrified to have her hand
not move at all and was then knocked unconscious
when whoever was holding onto her pulled her with
such force, she smashed her head into the wall and
went black.

The sound of a match being struck and the smell
of sulfur eased the girl's senses into consciousness.
She managed to keep her body still, trying to make
sense of where she was in the dark. Her head still
throbbed with a dull pain. She felt loose, scratchy
straw under her bare legs and tickling her neck. The
smell of wet stones was close. Her good ear perked up

as she heard someone walking around. The darkness turned to shadows and oranges and the stink of sulfur made her wrinkle her nose. When the little girl finally summoned the energy to turn her head, she saw the man sitting on a chair in front of her. Tavi moved her hands, bound at the wrists and looked to him, the candlelight dancing before her. Her mouth was dry and she felt like crying but she swallowed and managed to speak, her voice sounding less brave than she had hoped it would.

"Where…where am I?" The question bounced around the room in a way that made her feel small. A drip of water splashed to the ground, sounding louder than her question and she chewed her lip as she kept back her tears.

The man with the interesting boots chuckled, a low melodic laugh suggesting that she had just told a joke. He leaned forward on his chair, pressing his fingertips together and looking directly at her. His slicked back hair and scruffy face looked menacing in the dancing light. Deep blue eyes and angled features were familiar to her, roughened by a lack of a shave and fatigue showing in his face but not his eyes. This man had been coming to her mam all through the last three seasons and was a favorite of Prisca. He was able to conjure up whatever the girls needed and even brought Tavi something when she had pressed Prisca to ask him for it. It had been a pretty pin she had seen in the market, the head a shiny blue and white bead.

On occasion the girl had noticed the man watching her from time to time but Prisca had always guarded her from him, never letting Tavi keep him company if she wasn't there and instructing her not to answer any questions he put to her. His name was Derk and Prisca said he was well known among certain circles though 'The Lurk' disappeared when he needed to. He was here now. He brought the match to the pipe he held in his hands, pulling on it gently with a quiet breath. Tavi heard the tobacco crackling and the smoke tickled her nose when it reached her. He shook the match out before he flicked it to the floor. Even in the dark, his eyes were intense and he stared at her, pinning her down to the hay with his gaze. He crossed his arms over his chest and smiled faintly, the smoke of the pipe drifting off to nowhere. "Where do you think you are…Tavi, is it? Where do the dregs always wind up?"

Tavi drew her breath in sharply, her eyes wide with fright. The Jugs? Panic set in and her chest heaved as she started hyperventilating, worry squeezing at her tiny heart and lungs. Prison. He had caught her stealing from him and turned her in. Stories about the horrors of prison made her head hurt more. Loneliness, hunger, pain, the dangers of other prisoners. But she was just a little girl, wasn't she? Why would he turn her in? She hadn't taken anything, not really. But here she was, surrounded by stone and nothing but hay beneath her and the table before her. In front of her was a man who had knocked her unconscious with a flick of his wrist. Tavi wanted to scream. Her face felt hot and her stomach felt sick and something dripped down her forehead that felt like sweat. Fear made her whole body quake, dislodging the panic rumbling in her belly. When her mouth opened to scream, a shock of cold water slapped her in the face, dripping over her and soaking into her worn clothing. It snapped her brain away from her terror and the man shook her gently, his laughter sounding more nervous than comic this time.

"Come on now, I was only playing," he said, jostling the girl and smacking her lightly across the cheeks. Her mouth popped open like a fish as she gasped for air and cried, the remains of his bad joke drawing tears from her eyes. "It was only a joke," he said. He tried to meet her gaze but she looked away, still trembling so hard her teeth chattered, tears running down her cheeks. A rough hand brushed a tear away. "Hey, get a hold of yourself," he said, and it almost sounded gentle. "You're not in prison. Though you've a fear of the Jugs. Means you'll do your best to stay out of 'em. Means you'll do."

She was dropped back down onto the pile of hay, the man walking back to his chair to sit. Tavi took a moment to catch her breath, the shock of the horrible joke still causing her to shake. She felt so tired after being so afraid. Her head throbbed but her childish curiosity kept her from yielding to the weariness in her young body. "Do what?" she managed to say and this time it almost sounded like a demand and not a cry for help, kneeling in the hay. "What'll I do? And what did you do with mam? Did you hurt her?" For the first time she remembered Prisca and the shrill scream that was not her own before she went dark. "If you hurt her-"

"So, you've a bit of fire in your belly, as I thought." The man laughed again, reaching into his pack and pulling out something round, the other hand pulling out a small knife, the blade glinting in the scant light. "You'll do for me what you were doing for her, though more of it, and better eventually. No hiding behind walls and such. As for that woman you call 'mam,' who ain't your mother." He looked to her again, as if he was accusing her of something but Tavi shook it off, pressing her lips together. "Well, she's safe and sound."

"She'll want me back, you know, she'll come and get me," Tavi declared, her back as straight as she could hold it through her weariness, the ropes starting to dig into her wrists. Her head itched from the hay but she couldn't scratch it. The adrenaline surge that had come with her panic now sought to serve her in her assertion and she stood on her knees as tall as she could. "Y'can't keep me here. I'm hers, fair and square, I'm her girl. You'll have to take me back."

"Except that she gave you up, dear...Tavera. Tavera is your full name, right?" He cocked his head to the side, the light making the angles of his face sharper, more angular and she would have cowered if she wasn't trying to be brave at the moment. Derk let the round object in his hand into the light to reveal an apple, red and green on the outside with a leaf still attached to the stem. He cut a segment out of the fruit, bringing the white crescent to his mouth and took a bite of it, his face pensive as he quietly chewed. The smell of the apple mixed with the tobacco made her stomach rumble. He must have heard because he looked towards her. "She won't be looking for you, at least I don't suppose she shall. Seeing as how she gave you up to save her business."

What? Tavi felt as if her joints had gone cold and then melted, though her face was hot with shame and anger. Her head fell towards the hay to hide her face and she hoped it was too dark for him to see. "It…it ain't true, what you say…" she spoke down, into the hay. "She wouldn't do that. She…mam…."

"She loved you?" Derk made a sound and Tavera cringed. "I've been on the streets longer than you've been alive, little one, and I can assure you, no mam ever raised up her girl to lift her skirts for blueies and bits of ribbon. But I'm guessing you know nothing of proper mothers or fathers." He cut off another piece of the apple and ate it rather slowly, seeming to enjoy the piece of fruit. Then Derk stood up, walking slowly towards Tavi. His figure loomed in the balance between the light from the candle and the darkness of the room.

"But you've no need to worry, little Tavi. I've been watching you for quite some time and I know what you can do and I know what you'll be able to do." He said it quietly. It made Tavera turn her head to look up at him. His eyes were big, as if he were excited. "And, like a real father teaches his children, I intend to take it upon myself to teach you. No more picking pockets of poor saps and coming up with old scraps of fabric or rinds of cheese. No more stealing sausages off the spits and burning your fingers for what you foolishly deem a feast. I've a plan and an interest in you. And I can assure you, I won't be giving you up to no one. You're my girl, now, and I'm your pa."

He knelt down by the little girl, supporting her with one arm and bringing the apple up to her face. At first she didn't understand what he was doing but he pushed the apple towards her mouth. She could smell how sweet it was and finally she bit down into it, half expecting him to pull it away but hoping he wouldn't. He fed her the apple, not minding when the juice dripped onto his hand as she gobbled it down, the bit of food bracing her against her weariness. When the apple was done he threw the core away into a corner of the room and stood up, brushing his hands on his pants.

"Now, there's a party upstairs I am expected at and I don't want you there. It ain't for little girls." He wagged his finger at her as he said all this before he wiped his dagger on his pants, the blade disappearing within his clothes with the flick of a wrist. "I'm keeping you tied up for now but I'll be back soon. We'll leave tomorrow at the beginning of the first watch. Try to get some rest." He bowed to her in a comical way but his jest didn't make the little girl any less frightened. He chuckled when she didn't and grabbed his pipe and hat off the table.

"Wait! What if the candle goes out? Where're we goin' after this? Why are you doing this?" She threw all these questions at him as she forced herself up again. Her heart thumped in her small chest and the corners of the room seemed somewhat darker and more menacing as the man made to leave. Derk reached up and grabbed hold of a rope that hung down from the ceiling and pulled down a set of stairs, the light from above ground seeming warm and inviting. He turned towards her, putting the hat on his head and looked at her quizzically, a smirk on his mouth.

"You'll be asleep before the light goes out. As to where we're going, I'll know by the end of my party. And as to why…I don't feel like explaining now. I don't have to explain right now. But I swear by Her tits, it's for your own good." He bowed again, more deeply than before, so deep his hat fell off. Derk smiled as he picked it up, smacking it against his leg before he set it back on his head. Then he walked briskly up the steps, his boots making the same strange sound they had before.

For her own good? She trembled slightly as she laid herself down on the hay, trying to get comfortable with her hands behind her back. What he had said frightened her and excited her. Her own good? What did that mean? What one person called 'good' sometimes meant a different thing altogether. Prisca had said cutting all her hair off was for 'her own good.' Tavera's face grew hot again as she thought of Prisca. Hadn't she promised the girl she would take care of her? The woman had shared her bed with her, kept her warm, keeping her safe from the men who had asked after her, promised to teach her what she would need to know to make a man or a woman happy. Tavi swallowed the lump in her throat, sniffing to keep new tears from falling across her face.

She'd been sold before, so why would a prostitute's silly promises count for anything? Besides, Tavera told herself, her tongue darting out to lick up a salty tear, she didn't want to be a prostitute anyway. The dressing up, the make up, the bells, the peddling on the corners and steps of the temple…Tavera didn't like any of it. She didn't want to sell anything, let alone trade purses. She liked watching the people go by, trying to figure out where they were going, not trying to get them to come home with her. And though she did like taking from people and Prisca had encouraged it, Tavera felt like it was just another trick. Tavera was just another way for Prisca to get more out of her clients. When she asked questions, Prisca had always laughed at her.

The little girl felt her weariness well up suddenly, the candlelight fading slowly as her eyes fluttered closed, her thoughts making a final circle as they started to fade into dreams. Maybe things with Derk would be different. He said he would be her pa. Would it be any different from Prisca wanting to be her mam? She wouldn't know until he whisked her away from this life into the next and she remembered the way he had looked at her as he fed her the apple, the way he had bowed to her. Maybe he would love her and she would finally have just a bit of good in her life. Maybe he wouldn't use her and laugh at her. All the times she had encountered him before he didn't seem malicious or cruel. He smiled a lot and tried to help Prisca and the rest of the ladies. And he had gotten Tavi that pin. A smile curled the corners of her mouth as she settled into the hay. It didn't seem nearly as scratchy as it had before and before the candle wobbled three times before her drooping eyes, Tavera was fast asleep.

Chapter 2
A Contract of Emotion

Shortly after they arrived in the city of Southwick, the lessons began. The lessons were varied and were meant to teach different things. One of the first things The Lurk taught her was self-defense.

"Now I'm sure you've noticed by now that ladies and men have different parts to them," he said as he flicked the butt of his cigarette into the gutter, the acrid smell mixing with the stench of the open sewer. His shirt sleeves were rolled up and he set his booted feet firmly on the cobbled street, sniffling as he did. "Now this is where you've a bit of an advantage, Tavi dear. If any man grabs you for any reason and you want him off quick, just hit him betwixt and off he goes. Don't show any mercy or you're more likely to piss the man off. Grab, kick, bite if you have to but make it count and then run. If for some reason you can't reach 'em or you're up against a woman, a quick thump to the nose works as well." He lightly boxed her on the nose, tears welling up in her eyes making the alley seem like a blur of browns and blacks for just a few breaths. "But much harder," he said. "Try to draw more than tears."

In Greyhollow they stayed in a room above a tavern. Tavi was given the bed with the warm blankets and if Derk ever minded sleeping in the chair by the door, he never complained. The stairs leading down to the tavern creaked no matter how lightly they stepped and the Lurk was always very kind to the tender he called Brags. Derk introduced Tavi to him as Kiffer. This had made the old man cleaning glasses with a dirty rag laugh and he offered her an apple from behind the bar every time he saw her. Tavi always took it and as Derk had instructed her, thanked him, trying her best to answer to the new name her father had bestowed upon her.

"You must be careful not to shit where you eat, Tavi," he said one day as he was rolling a cigarette. He had acquired a lock from somewhere and Tavera was trying to pick it, inserting the pin he bought her all those phases ago and a filed nail into the keyhole, fiddling them around, her tongue sticking out the side of her mouth as she tried to feel with metal fingers. Derk licked the paper and gazed over to gauge her progress, reaching over to light the cigarette in the lantern as he finished his thought. "Few people will truly deserve your kindness but if they do, give it to them. In the line of work we're in, few trust us, though many more falsely say they do. When you move about a lot, a friendly face is worth more than a grip of blues." He took a pull of the smoke just as Tavera's mouth and the lock popped open. Derk smiled at her while Tavera beamed, her small, skinny hands shaking with excitement. "Very good, Tavi," he said.

It was from Derk that she learned her numbers and her letters. After most lessons, Derk would light his pipe, sit upon the nearest thing he could sit upon and say, "Now take care to recall this, as there'll be a test." This distressed Tavera greatly and finally one afternoon, after another self-defense bout that actually left Derk with a bloody nose, she admitted she had no knowledge of cipher or script. "Tits of ivory, you can't write or do figures?" He laughed incredulously, bright red blood trickling from his nose so that it dripped onto his shirt. Only after a bit of time did he finish laughing and then he cleaned up properly and put his arm around her, grabbing his pack on the way out of the alley. "I shouldn't be surprised, not like whores need instructions to get it done. Toss a bottle down an alley, and it's over."

Tavera stiffened at his words. Her thoughts of Prisca resurfaced and a lump formed in her throat as she thought of the time she had spent with Prisca and how the woman had betrayed her. It still stung, raw in her memory like a scab that had been pulled off. Derk squeezed her shoulder reassuringly and led her down the street, holding her to him in something like a hug. "Come now, don't think upon her, she can't hurt you anymore," he said in an attempt to comfort her, somehow knowing what she was thinking. "You're with me now." He carried her to a small shop and bought her a tablet and some chalks to learn letters. They used coins the Lurk had won at gambling to study numbers and values, learning the conversions of half blueies to blueies to fullies. Tavera was much better at the numbers than the letters, much to Derk's delight and chagrin.

Some of the lessons were harder, closer to Tavera's old life but necessary. One morning he announced that he wouldn't buy her any food for a phase and unleashed her on the streets. Tavera roamed the markets for an entire watch, looking over her shoulder for the blond thief that was supposed to be training her. Food danced out in the corner of her eye, taunting her. The little girl watched carefully, sniffing the air, dark eyes set not on the food making her mouth water but on those manning the food carts and stalls. Her stomach gurgled, not to the point of distraction but sharp enough to make her senses keen, honing the movements that drew her closer to her target, conserving her energy for both stealth and speed. At the most opportune moment, when her ears buzzed with excitement but when able to best control it, she struck, small hands and wiry fingers darting out, skinny legs walking casually to where she would be able to enjoy her food in peace. Her heart thumped in her chest as she walked, faster than her normal pace and Tavi tried her best to keep from giggling with excitement.

One day after acquiring a rather delicious piece of fish, she turned the corner only to walk right into the Lurk, smashing into him so that she shouted in surprise and fell back. The ground was hard and Tavi winced as she fell onto her backside, tears springing to her eyes with pain. Derk picked up the piece of fish and sniffed it rather thoughtfully, running it under his nose like one of the cigarettes he was always rolling. Tavera narrowed her eyes at him for once while she pressed her lips together, arms crossed over her belly meant to dampen the sound of her growling stomach.

"This is what you have going for you now, Tavera dear, and listen to me," he started, and she recognized the tone he always used when he was going to point something out. "You don't stand out. Many children are obnoxious and call attention to themselves. They tug on skirts and caterwaul. They cry for food, as if they deserve it. I imagine misfortune has made this path unavailable to you as a way to get what you need, but you have turned necessity into a gift. When one looks upon you, they see a sad waif. Nothing special, even with your ear and that skin of yours that hints at something else. Floating about sadly, most likely to wind up adrift in the gutters some day, that's what people see, those that don't know any better. And then you strike and they're none the wiser." Derk was smiling though his words weren't kind. They made Tavera's face hot and she bit her lip, wondering what he was getting it. She knew better than to interrupt him and waited as he gestured, completing his speech, her ear perking up to take it all in. "This will work for now," he continued, "while you're young and skinny and pathetic looking. But what happens when those years of change come?" Blue eyes looked her over and Tavera made a face at him, trying to shoo his gaze away, which made him laugh. "You're not much to look at now but I've seen plenty ugly little girls grow up to have looks that destroy men's egos and burn through purses. People will be watching you. Not now but once you've grown some, you will have eyes upon you. Please, keep this in mind.

"Which brings me to another point," Derk said, sniffing the fish again, the girl's mouth watering as she thought about how good it would taste, the tender, smoky flesh tinged with just the right amount of salt, the crunchy bits she would save for last. He eyed the girl for a few breaths before he went on, dangling the fish in front of her. "Watch your Ws. We're thieves, and fine ones. Well, I'm a fine one and you're only my student for now. Stupid thieves, sloppy thieves, lazy ones turn the same tricks all the time. In through the window, out the back door, blade to the purse strings.

"Do not let this get boring and always learn or be willing to do so. Change it all the time or the seat-and-sworders will have a set of bracelets on you before the fun is over. To be unstoppable you must be unpredictable and un…well, when I think of the word, I'll tell you." Tavi stuck her tongue out at him and tried to grab the fish but he pulled it away at the last second and laughed, grinning at her. "And by Her luminous breasts, get away from the guards before they have you by the wrists in metal. Not because you won't be able to get out of them but because it's better they think you're a common criminal rather than know who you really are. Or in your case, what you're going to be." At this, he ripped the fish carefully in two and handed one of the pieces to Tavi, eating his portion gingerly and never speaking if his mouth was full of food. She gobbled hers up, considering his words as she chewed and gulped, not bothering to save any of it for later. When she was done eating, he gave her a handful of last year's dried ground apples for a treat.

Derk introduced her to a variety of colorful figures, calling them by names that couldn't possibly be their real ones. Tavi soon learned though he was acquainted with all the men he introduced her to (as Kiffer), he knew some men better than others, to the point where he actually knew their given names. These names were never spoken in public and rarely in private company. It was in Brags' bar that she met

Snitch Bigguns, a man with a giant nose and an ego to match. Merl was handy with cards and often called upon when a joke was in order, an expert in diffusing a tense situation. Vamp the Lipper possessed a fine, falsetto singing voice that never hinted at the beatings the man could deliver when provoked. All these men and more knew the Lurk and delighted in the Kiffer. They plied her with treats and blueies, gave her sips of their drinks and asked her when she would be kind enough to play snakesman for them.

"What's the Cup of Cream?" she asked the Lurk one afternoon as they sat in the bar. The taste of the watered down stout Brags served children still danced on her tongue and the dark brown foam fizzled above her mouth. Derk quickly scanned the room before he turned his eyes back on her and took out his pocket handkerchief, leaning over the table and wiping her mouth before setting the hanky on the table top and smiling.

"So, you do catch on," he said, lacing his fingers around the mug of beer. He turned in his seat slightly so that his body cheated away from the rest of Brags' clientèle before he took a long sip and peered at Tavi, keen blue eyes staring into her. "Do you remember the little trick I played on you, when we first met? Remember what I said?"

Tavi frowned slightly, her large mouth still wet with beer. It hadn't been a funny trick, she thought, remembering how she had been tied up, the pain in her head, the fright. But it had been a trick, part of it. Everything since that night had been fine, better than her life before. The soothsayers words had been meant for Tavera, not Prisca. Tavi knew that now. The half elf girl enjoyed the instructions she received from Derk and the smiles she received from him when she succeeded made her smile more often than not. There was a wish to make him happy and so she tried to think of what he had told her that night, blinking. She pushed a streak of hair out of her face and shrugged. "The dregs…the dregs wind up in the Jugs."

"And what does cream do?" he asked, leaning over slightly, his voice low and even. Tavera leaned back in her seat, gulping slightly as she tried to think of the right thing to say.

"It…it rises to the top." She was fairly certain that this was the answer and the smile playing behind Derk's eyes told her she was right. He nodded, leaning over the table again, this time to tussle her hair.

"Right you are, Tavi dear. The Cream always rises to the top. The Dregs fall to the bottom. And we, well I am part of the Cream, me and my mates. If you keep going the way you're going, you'll be up there with us. We're a small club, tight knit though some knots are tighter than others, if you catch my meaning. Not everyone I show you off to is in on it, but you'll soon be able to piece it out or you'll have to. Just ask me when we're alone, you and I, if you ain't sure." He drummed his fingers on the tabletop and looked around, a bit of nervousness showing in his face for the very first time. As soon as Tavera saw it the look was gone and his eyes were on her again, the tone of a teacher back in his words. "That's another thing you should learn, when to ask questions, what kinds of questions to ask, things of that nature. By Her heaving chest, I should be writing this all down and keeping track, now, shouldn't I?"

The most important of the early lessons Derk the Lurk taught Tavera was not meant to be a lesson at all. One cold evening he sent Tavera off with a few coins to the Fence to buy him some of the tobacco he liked so much, telling her to be quick as he was almost out. The little girl cut through the alleys, running over the cobbled streets as quickly as she could, trying to outrun the stench of decay and refuse that permeated this particular part of town. Her footsteps echoed in the barren streets, making the city at night seem bigger than it actually was. Turning a corner, an arm darted out and grabbed a hold of her, twisting her arm backwards before she could react. The coins fell to the ground, clinking melodiously as a filthy hand covered her mouth, callouses rendering her teeth useless, her small frame lifted off the ground.

Tavera tried to scream, twisting and writhing in her attacker's arms but her attempts to escape drew his sordid frame around her tighter, almost crushing. It was dark in the alley, the dim lantern light of the

main street seeming to back away from her as she
kicked, one of her boots flying off of her feet. Nails
dug into her and horrible words hissed in her ear. The
words were terrible and drew muffled shrieks from
her throat, hot tears of protest forming in her eyes.
Then there was a whistling sound, a jerk and suddenly
she was released. Tavi fell to the ground, crying out as
the sharp rocks pounded into her bare knees, gasping
as she tried to breathe. She turned around to see what
happened and saw a filthy man with green rotten
teeth and calloused hands lying on his back, blood
gurgling from his mouth. Out of the shadows stepped
two figures: one hooded and wearing a long, green
scarf, his gloved hands wielding a crossbow. The
other was Derk, his eyes two points of blue fire set in a
face of stone. The fingers on his right hand moved
and a dagger produced itself out of thin air, the two
men walking past her and circling around her as-
sailant.

Derk said something that she couldn't make out
but the air seemed to burn with words of intense,
concentrated hatred. He spat to the side, the man in
the hood matching his gait, cocking the crossbow
back so loudly it made her jump. The man on the
ground arched his back and Tavera could see the remnants of a bolt in his back, his blood mingling with
the slick wetness of the cobblestones. The man blub-
bered something about a misunderstanding, that he
was only playing and the little girl was overreacting to

a joke. He gasped in pain, the milky whites of his eyes shining as Derk and the stranger stood over him, the dagger glinting and its light seeming to whisper a prophecy in the dark. Tavera drew in her breath as the light of the dagger disappeared and then glowed once more, darker, redder, dripping with a slowing tempo as the man on the ground wheezed and then stopped moving.

"Worthless," Derk said, looking up to his comrade, nodding to him quickly. "Many thanks, Jezlen," he said, turning his attention to the little girl. The dagger was still dirty with the dead man's blood, but his eyes had softened. His empty hand reached out towards her. "Tavera," he said quietly. "Tavera, are you alright? Did he hurt you?"

Tavi managed to shake her head but found her legs unable to work. She wouldn't cry, she told herself, holding back the whimpers that threatened to erupt into tears. Derk stepped over the body and walked up to her, scooping her up into his arms.

"I'm sorry, Derk," she said, crying into his shoulder, wrapping her arms around his neck. She buried her face into his coat and cloak, the tears coming anyway and soaking them through as she sobbed. "I tried to do what you told me but he picked me up so fast, I couldn't do nothing, I'm sorry." He shushed her gently telling her it wasn't her fault and he understood.

"What now, Dershik?" For a moment Tavera wondered who the hooded man was talking to, her eyes setting upon Derk as she realized that the hooded man was talking to him. Dershik must be his real name and Jezlen must in the Cup, she thought. Dershik, or Derk the Lurk shrugged, wiping his blade on the dead man's clothes, clutching the girl to him tightly.

"I doubt anyone will miss this sorry hem-chewer. Find her boot, will you?" he said. Still holding Tavera to him with one arm, he pulled out his flask, unscrewed the lid with his teeth and poured it over the already stinking body. "We're off to Portsmouth, if you need us."

Tavera could swear she could see a smile gleam from within the hood, the fellow uncocking his crossbow and holstering it within his cloak. The other man walked a few steps down the alley and bent down, picking her boot up off the ground and handing it over to Derk. "Portsmouth, eh?" he said. His voice had a strange accent to it, though there was also mirth in his words. Tavera wondered where he was from. "I hear Celeel is there."

"Old Gam? Yah don't say?" The way Derk said it made Tavera think that he knew this woman was there and she saw the other man narrow his eyes at Derk while Derk just wagged his eyebrows at him. "Well maybe I'll pop by for a smoke and a bit to show off little Tavi. What say you?" Tavera looked up, large eyes meeting Derk's, her large mouth still in a rather pathetic pout but her eyes void of tears. He kissed her soundly on the forehead, the first time he had done so, before he slipped her boot back onto her foot. Holding onto her firmly he stretched his free arm towards his friend.

"Take care of yourself and the little one," Jezlen said and the two men shook hands, finally falling into something like an embrace. The man was careful not to touch Tavera. "And tell Old Gam I still dislike her."

"She still dislikes you, I'm sure of it." Derk turned and they left. When Tavera looked down the alley, Jezlen was gone but the body was still there, lifeless. The rats were already scurrying out of the shadows to claim their share.

Derk, Dershik, her adopted father. He had killed a man to protect her. There was something frightening about knowing this but something comforting, a kind of peace that seemed to envelope them both as they walked down alleys, coming to a stable. The danger was gone but the ordeal had made Tavera tired, the words Derk exchanged with the stableman lost to her. They both mounted a single horse, Derk setting Tavera on the saddle in front of him and taking the reigns himself. Her mind wandered as the horse walked quietly out of the city through the night, taking the man and little girl with him. Derk was her father and she knew it now. He had done something heroic to save her, been there in her time of need. Isn't that what a father was? Someone to protect her when she needed protecting? Someone to be there for her? Someone to love her enough to do so. The steady rhythm of the horse's motion was soothing and she could feel Derk's heart beating in his chest. She smiled as she cuddled closer to the man who wrapped his cloak around her protectively and Tavera felt warm and comfortable, both inside and out. "I love you, poppa," she said quietly. The moon peeked out from behind some trees, lighting their way and Tavera wrapped her small hands around the reins as well, wondering what the next town held for them.

Chapter 3
First Impressions

The deadbolt slid back, the door opened and Tavera peered up expectantly at the woman who stood in the doorway. Confusion tweaked at the little girl's eyebrows as she considered the woman who smirked at Derk and then looked down blankly at her. Derk was grinning at this woman who wasn't 'Old' at all. Her hair was brown and fell in soft curls around her rather round face and her skin was smooth, not wrinkled. The woman called both 'Celeel' and 'Old Gam' turned and walked into the apartment with a slight roll of her eyes, Derk giving Tavi a quick squeeze on the shoulder before they entered.

"I's hoping that the rumors were just that," the woman said, her back turned towards them. Tavi gazed around the two roomed home, various belongings piled and set around in a way that said it was in fact a home and not another room above a bar. A table and two chairs were the focus of the front room, an embroidered cloth draped over the tabletop. The chairs didn't match in style but the wood was the same hue. One of them was pulled out and a bit of sewing lay on the seat, half done. Quilts hung on the wall across from the only window and a small fire burned in the fireplace, no doubt keeping whatever was in the black pot warm.

Derk closed the door behind them and locked it, pulling off his hat and the face he was making at Tavera suggesting that she take off her outdoor clothes. "Rumors are always founded on some bit of truth, you should know that. You of all people."

"So what are the lies and what are the truths, Derk?" Tavera decided that Celeel had a warm smile but that it was weary and the little girl felt as if it was a smile she only had for Derk. "Have you eaten?" she asked them both, not waiting for him to answer. "It ain't good to not eat, 'specially when you're little." She looked over at Tavera over her shoulder as she fiddled with something on a smaller table that was kept by the fire. "How old are you?"

Tavera just shrugged. She looked at Derk to see what he thought of the answer she had given and he just scratched his head, visibly uncomfortable. Celeel laughed, something between a chuckle and a cackle. "The two of you…eh?" She shook her head.

"Aye, the two of us." He pulled off his cloak and hung it on the back of the door before he moved the sewing and sat on the chair. The smile he tried to give Tavera was probably meant to be reassuring but all she could do was stand there and frown, not sure what to do.

Old Gam looked at her again. "What, is she mute? I've heard otherwise but as long as she ain't deaf, no harm done."

"She's not mute," Derk sighed. Blue eyes looked over the bit of sewing he had put on the table and he poked at it, grimacing at the stain he left with his finger. He tried to rub it out and shot a glance at Tavi, looking guilty and amused at the same time. Tavi pressed her lips together and tried not to laugh as well, her small hands covering her mouth.

"You ain't going to throw up, right? I hear small ones do that." Old Gam said. She walked to the table with three plates, setting them down before she noticed the bit of stitching, Derk looking to the side as he tried to avoid what was soon turning into a glare on her face. The woman just sighed and shook her head, disappearing into the other room while Tavi finally decided to take off her cloak. She had to jump to get it up on the peg but reached it on her third try, glad she didn't tear the garment on the peg as her feet hit the floor. Tavera heard Old Gam walking back into the room and the little girl felt her ears burn while she walked to the empty seat, sitting in front of the plate the woman had been kind enough to make for her.

"An apprentice," Old Gam said. She almost sang it and it made Tavera stare into her plate harder. It was cold roasted fish and barley cakes, with sweet onion paste to moisten the bread. Her stomach rumbled.

"What, food and no drink?" Derk asked. For a second there was silence in the room, though the sounds of Portsmouth could be heard beyond the walls, keeping it from being too quiet. Whatever Old Gam was sitting on scraped against the wooden floor as she pushed it back, Tavera stealing a glance at her pa. He was smiling at her again and he winked, tearing a bit of bread and fish and dipping it into the jelly before he licked his fingers. Old Gam returned to the table with a jug and two mugs.

"I only have the two," she said, setting one in front of herself and Derk, pouring what was probably the local thinny into his glass.

"It's alright, I'll let her have the last bit of mine when I'm done," he offered, watching as she filled the mug. He picked it up as soon as she pulled the jug away, taking a big swig. "Ah, refreshing. You get this from Three Fingers?"

"Two Fingers, now. Dar got him for a digit three phases ago."

"Who cares? His wife says he's better with his tongue anyway. And his beer's still the best in Portsmouth."

"I'd rather have all my fingers," Tavera finally said, frowning slightly. Old Gam and Derk both looked at her and for a moment she thought she had said something wrong but they both started laughing. Tavi shoved a bit of food in her mouth while they laughed, wondering what was so funny.

"By Her hems, Derk, what do you think you're doing with her?" Old Gam finally asked, rubbing her brow with her hand. Tavera took another mouthful, wondering who Old Gam was talking about it and she swallowed, realizing it was her.

"Everything you've heard I've been doing with her," Derk said, and it was almost a hiss. He tore another piece of bread off and gestured at Tavera with it. "Come on, Celeel. It's not a bad idea."

"It's a terrible idea. Firstly, she's a child. Secondly, she looks nothing like you. You can't even lie and say she's your kin. Plus she's part Forester. What could be more memorable than a blond loudmouth and a half Forester girl that looks nothing like him gallivanting through Her creation?"

"A child is easier to train than an adult and she'd already shown ability before I took her."

"Oh, so you were watching her before you made her your little chick. How very sweet, stalking children."

"I was NOT stalking her. I noticed her."

"Did you happen to notice her coloring? Does she remind you of anyone?" Gam's voice lilted when she asked and Derk stared into his cup, sitting low in his chair when she did. "Dark hair, that pretty skin. Eyes are off, but anyone that knew-"

"Shut up," Derk said. He was gripping his cup so hard that his knuckles were white and red, his voice as icy as his eyes. He looked to Old Gam and any other person would have been frightened by the look he was giving her. Old Gam just looked...sad. Derk cleared his throat and took a sip of his beer, still staring into it. "Tavi doesn't look like...her. At all. I would know, of all people." He set his eyes on Tavera now, as if to make sure what he said was true and she stared back, not sure who she was supposed to not look like. He leaned over the table and offered the cup to Tavi and a smile managed to poke at the corners of his mouth, trying to chase away the seriousness in the room.

"Besides that...what else did you say? Ah, yes." Derk turned his attention to his plate and set the rest of his fish on his bread, piling the onions on top. "There are plenty of mixed families in The Valley. We wouldn't be the first mismatched family members to trample the Crescents. And the ears...well, only one is a giveaway. Easily covered by her hair once it's longer, or a cloak. The skin, working in the sun too long. Some Valleymen are given to a darker coloring." He took a bite of his food, several of the onions sliding off and onto his chin, making her pa set his food down to clean his face.

"Fine, so you have a little girl to teach, to tell all your stories to, to get your breakfast for you," Old Gam said. She squinted at Tavera and the little girl could feel her eyes set on her ear, the one that had been cut and her fingers went up instinctively, covering it with her dark hair. "To what end, Derk? Why?"

"I thought that was the most obvious," Derk said, eating the last of his food. He chewed and swallowed, wiping his hands on his pants before he burped quietly into a fist. "She's to be my apprentice."

"Did you start making hats behind my back, Derk?"

"And one day," he huffed, ignoring her joke, "she'll be in the Cup." Now he looked to Tavi, raising his blond eyebrows at her hopefully. A smile tugged at her mouth and she took a sip of the beer, finding it flat but tasty. Old Gam was looking at her, she knew it.

"One day," Old Gam said. "If she has any skill. And the desire. And if she gets people to vouch for her." Tavi could hear Old Gam breathing, slow and measured as if trying not to get angry. "She knows about The Cup?"

"She asked me about it!" Derk insisted. "I ran into Walik in Greyhollow and we got to talking. I'm telling you, she's sharp! The Lipper was there too and she pieced it all out. She's a sharp ear...no pun intended. Tavi pays attention, she's good with her hands, she's fast, she's small so she can get in and out of spots. And that's now! Give her a handful of years and she'll outshine even me!"

"What does Jezlen think of all this?" Old Gam took her plate and Derk's, Tavi still working on her portion. Derk just snuffed, digging in his bag. Tavi knew he was looking for his pipe and he found it, pulling it out of his pack with a tug, poking the bowl with his finger.

"Since when do you care what Jezlen thinks?" Derk asked, trying to find his tobacco. Tavera shoved the rest of her food in her mouth and chewed, drinking her drink to make it go down easier. "Tavi, don't shove so much in your mouth, you'll choke," he said, pointing at her with his pipe.

"You are the proud papa, aren't you?" Old Gam snickered. This time she came back with her mug and a bottle of something else, steam rising from the mug. "So, what does the big elf think about the little elf?"

"Well," Derk started. He pushed the tobacco into his pipe and stood up from the table, walking over to the fireplace for a light. The fire colored him orange and he plucked a smoldering stick from the fire and set his pipe. "At first, he thought I was crazy."

"So…Jezlen thinks you're crazy. And you still took her on?"

Jezlen. Jezlen was the man who had helped her father save her from her attacker. He had the crossbow and the scarf across his face and grey eyes. He had seemed sympathetic towards her then, called her 'little one.' But she knew that Jezlen and Old Gam didn't like each other. The two men had joked about it while she clung to Derk, trying to dry her tears and snot on his shoulder. He had seemed kind. Derk's stories said otherwise. The elf was frustrating beyond all belief and sounded crazy though all the stories Derk told of him ended in laughter. That was the way things were, supposedly. In the end, you looked back at them and laughed. So far nothing in Tavera's life made her laugh, though a few memories made her smile. Most of them had been made with Derk in their short stint together.

"First of all, I didn't just 'take her on' as you keep on saying. I've adopted her. As my daughter."

"Have you taken vows before the Goddess?"

"What?" Derk puffed on the pipe and the sweet, herbal smoke was starting to fill the room. "No, we didn't take vows. D'you think that's smart, me going into a temple and having four priestesses bear witness to me and her starting a family? She's been with me for less than seven phases, and I don't need a priestess to bear witness to my intentions with Tavera."

"And what are your intentions with Tavera?"

"Have you been paying attention this whole time, Gam?" Derk squinted at her as if she were stupid and they locked eyes on each other, another gulp of silence filling the room. "I am going to raise her as my daughter, I am going to teach her to be a better thief and she will eventually become a member of the Cup. They won't be able to turn her down."

"You don't know that for sure, Derk," Old Gam said. "And besides, what father raises his daughter to be a thief?"

"What parent doesn't wish for their child to follow in their footsteps?"

"How many parents are thieves?"

"More than would admit it, Celeel." Another pause filled the room and Tavera finished her drink, wondering how long Old Gam and Derk had known each other, that they could talk without talking. It must have been a long time indeed because the silence dragged on and Derk puffed on his pipe in an irritated way. Tavera was starting to pick up on what anger did to Derk's face and it was there, making his eyes dark and his face tight. The little girl could feel her stomach fluttering, as if the fish had come back to life as nervousness rose in her belly. What if Old Gam was right? What if the Cup of Cream wouldn't take her? And if Derk realized that now, what would happen to her? He had rescued her twice now but he hadn't made any vows, had he? Tavera didn't want to start crying, not here in this woman's eating room. Old Gam's opinion obviously mattered and she couldn't have the woman thinking she was meant for swaddling clothes. So the girl just stared at the cloth that was on the table, trying to think about something else.

"What does Hock think about all this?"

"Tits, so many hemming questions!" Derk

shouted. He threw his hands in the air and walked to the door, grabbing his cloak.

"Where's you going?" Tavera asked as loudly as she could manage, a touch of panic making her sit straight up in her seat. Derk fastened his cloak about his neck and pulled the hood up, looking to Gam with a bit of ire still in his eyes.

"Night prayers," he said, pulling back the latch on the door. "I'll be back before bed, don't worry." He gave Old Gam another look of anger before he opened the door with a yank, letting it slam behind him.

Tavera felt her guts unravel within her as fear stuck in her throat. But Old Gam chuckled and said, "Good, he's gone. Now it's just us girls." Tavera looked at her, frowning, not understanding for a moment but Old Gam winked at her. Tavera pressed her lips together, not sure what to expect from Old Gam. The woman cleared her plate and picked up her sewing, sitting in Derk's seat and looking over the bit of needlework. "Do you know how to sew?" she asked, not bothering to look up.

Tavera just shook her head and Old Gam shook hers and made a sound with her tongue against her teeth in disapproval. "You should learn. It's good to know how to do many things. Besides snatch." Now Old Gam looked at her, brown eyes looking at the little girl almost kindly. "Besides, Derk is not exceedingly handy with a needle and thread. You should take care to learn." She stood up and dug around in the box she had been sitting on and pulled out a needle, thread and piece of fabric, taking the few steps she needed to set them before Tavera. "Maybe you can make a little pillow or something. For a doll."

"I ain't got no dolls," Tavera said, staring down at the items helplessly. Her hands were still a bit greasy and she wiped them on her skirt, Old Gam making another sound of disapproval.

"No dolls? And how has he got you dressed? Stand up now!" Tavera huffed before she stood up, hands together and held in front of her. She could manage to hold her head up at least and she did, looking at the woman. Closer up Tavi could see freckles on Old Gam's face. Stray curls hinted with blond and no make up made Gam's features warm and natural. Her brown eyes looked the little girl over. There was a bit of humor in them and a bit of disapproval. "Your hair's too short. But he found you that way, didn't he?" Tavera nodded, not wanting to admit the reason why her hair had been shorn all those phases ago lest the woman fear for her own hair. "An ash-dyed dress. If you knew how to sew, you could have prettier clothes, like me. Like all little girls want." Tavera just shrugged in reply. She didn't mind the clothes she had. They were warm and they mostly fit. It was big around the middle so many a snatched item had made its way into the top, stopped by a simple sash tied above where her hips would eventually be.

"Plus you could turn one dress into another piece altogether. A bit of lace, a ribbon. Maybe a dip in dye if you have the time." Tavera noticed the needlework around the neckline of Old Gam's dress. Starbloom danced along the edges of the fabric, the stitches in what had once been white. "This dress used to be barley brown and now look." The dress was blue now, much to Tavera's surprise. She knew that people dyed fabric to make it different colors. Sheep and goats only came in a few colors but never in blue or green or yellow. "There's more to taking than just taking, is what I'm trying to tell you, little one," Old Gam said, pushing the sewing towards her again, gesturing for her to sit down. Tavera sat down with a thump, knocking the sewing off the table as she did. "There's transforming, there's changing over. Quickly and with the right people." She handed the sewing back to Tavera. "See if you can sew a circle, dear." Tavera looked down at the fabric, wondering how she was going to lay it flat.

"D'you have something to...keep the cloth tight?" Tavera asked, holding the needle in her hand. Old Gam smiled and set her own work down, retreating into the back room for a moment. Tavera noticed she didn't bring a light into the room and figured the woman knew the layout of the chamber and its contents by heart. The woman opened something large and moved things around, returning with two wooden hoops, one slightly smaller than the other.

She took the fabric from Tavera and laid it over the smaller hoop, pushing the larger hoop over the fabric to keep it in place. The corners of Tavera's mouth lifted slightly, seeing the fabric laid out before her, imagining the circle that could be.

"So, you can smile?" Old Gam said, laughing. She sat back down, arranging her skirts under her before she took up her work again, sewing quickly as she spoke. "It's also important to have the right tools. It's good that you asked for the hoop, Tavera. No point in making things harder for yourself. If there's a tool, use it. The Goddess knows that Derk uses them when he can. He stole some tools of mine once. Never bothered trying to replace them, did he. Rummaged through my things and when I awoke, they were both gone."

They both sat there sewing for a few breaths, Tavera watching Old Gam's hands occasionally as she thought about what Old Gam said about Derk and trying to figure out why she said it. Derk had spoke positively of Old Gam on their way to Portsmouth but in their short conversation she had been harsh with him, trying to get him to leave. For what? To get Tavera alone to see if she could sew a circle? Tavera squinted her eyes and drew the thread up, careful to leave a tail so as not to undo her work.

"Do you know what being in the Cup of Cream is all about, Tavera? Or Kiffer? He calls you that sometimes, right?" They both kept sewing and Tavera imagined the circle in the fabric, pushing the needle through and up again.

"It's about taking things and being happy about taking them. It's about being the best," Tavi said finally. She was halfway done with the circle.

"And it's about getting rid of the worst." Tavera nodded at Old Gam's words though to be honest, she wasn't sure exactly what that meant. Derk had mentioned it but never laid out who 'the worst' really was. During their phases together she had seen him deal with some characters that might be considered the worst, laughing with them, playing cards with them, buying their drinks and cheating them out of their money. He used them as lessons for her, telling her who to watch for what, asking her what she noticed about them and rewarding her with a piece of dried fruit or a treat if she caught something exceedingly difficult. When she noticed that Dip bit his bottom lip when he was considering bolting for the door, she was given a whole blueie to spend on whatever she wanted. She still had it, tucked into her boot. It wasn't the best place to hide it, she knew. But at least it was hidden.

"Weak animals are always culled from the herd," Old Gam said. She could look at Tavera and sew at the same time which made Tavera's ear perk, impressed. "Too many fleas and the dog will scratch. Do you understand?" Tavera heard the questions and she thought she understood. Skinny little fingers pushed the needle through the fabric and back through.

"So…the Cup also gets rid of bad takers. But…." Tavera's large mouth frowned, a question forming in her young mind. "If they's only good takers, won't the law take notice? And answer them, skill for skill?"

Old Gam laughed again, her laugh that was a mixture of a chuckle and a cackle, reaching over and pushing Tavera's hair behind her good ear. "You are smart, aren't you?" Old Gam stopped before she said something, Tavera saw it on her mouth and in her eyes but she held back. "The key is balance," she continued, going back to her needlework. "If there were only excellent takers scheming in the cellars and bars of the Valley they would all fight among themselves and yes, you're right. The swordholders would notice and have to act accordingly. The locks would get better, the risks would be higher which some wouldn't mind. But the fact of the matter is, there will always be other kinds of takers. Some are middling good, some aren't half bad, some are terrible. And they all have their reasons. Some need to feed their families and are forced to take. They generally stick to food, things they can easily sell. Some take for others. They work for other people, for someone else's pocket." Again, Old Gam paused, letting the statement hang in the air. Tavera felt as if it were supposed to bother her but it didn't. The little girl kept on sewing, her circle almost complete.

"And some do it for themselves. Because it's fun." That was why Tavera took, more than for need. That's what had pushed Tavera's little hand forward that first time ever. She hadn't been hungry and the street vendor was closing up, putting the unsold tarts away into a crate to take home. The market day had been winding down and so the amount of people on the street was starting to dwindle.

As always, no one seemed to notice the little girl with the greasy black hair so she waited till he had space for three more tarts in the crate before she started walking towards the stand, reaching for it right when he had turned around to put the little crate on the cart, the filling smashing into her palm as she grabbed it and walked as steadily away as she could, the pace of her legs slower than the thumping in her chest. Prisca asked her where she had gotten it but Tavi shrugged and offered it to her in order to divert her questions. But the first time had led to a second and a third and soon Prisca caught on and showed her the little crawl space in the room.

"Yes, there's the thrill. Probably one of the few kinds of thrills you can have, being your age." Old Gam smirked at this and gave her a look, a look that Prisca had given her sometimes when bringing up her age. "But it's only thrilling if you don't get caught, little one. Get chased but don't get caught. Ever. Let the bad ones get caught, to keep the brown cloaks happy, to make them think they're doing their job just right. The sloppy ones, the cruel ones, let them all have their turn in the dregs. The worst. They ruin it for everyone, my dear. Not just people like Derk and I." The woman's hands stopped moving and she smoothed the fabric out, looking it over, a stray brown curl falling into her face. "Tell me, Tavera, who is the worst person you know?"

Tavera stopped sewing. She was a few stitches from being done but the question was put to her and she had to think about it. Plenty of people had been mean to her but she hadn't received the worst treatment out of all the people she had met in her short life. She still had all her fingers and toes. She heard some block lords sometimes took them from people who owed debts. Maybe the man who had taken her from her father was the worst, though she didn't know his name. And she barely recalled her own father's face. Did that make her the worst person she knew? A little girl who couldn't remember her blood father's face?

"Who cut your ear?" Old Gam asked. Tavera tightened up as the question shot through her, sharp as any knife and just as cold. She pressed her lips together and stared down at the circle she had sewn, just two stitches needed to finish it. Old Gam placed her sewing on the table and she put her hands on the edge of her own skirts, lifting them up to show a pale leg. Fine brown hair grew on her skin and several moles dotted it but as she pulled up the garment, a large, pink scar appeared, the remnants of a burn long healed but still ugly. Tavera wasn't sure if she was supposed to look away or not but she felt compelled to stare.

"When I was born," Old Gam said, breaking the spell of the horrible scar but still holding Tavera's attention. "I had a birthmark on my leg. It covered my whole thigh and it was blue, believe it or not, or so I recall. Probably closer to purple. In any case, my pa was a very strange man with strange ideas which is why he moved my ma and me and my little sister to the Freewild shortly after she was born. A holy man, he called himself. Sent by the goddess Herself to rid the Valley of the taint of the evil ones. Mind you, he most loudly proclaimed this when he'd drank a bit of the goddess' gift, if you hear me.

"Well, my pa started to say that I was marked for evil. The birthmark was proof of it and he went on to say my mother must have done something to taint the offspring so. He went on and on, condemning us, shaking things at us. Sometimes he built fires in the forest and danced around them under the moon in self styled robes. We heard about it from the other villagers. Other times he would leave us, to rid himself of us evil ones. Sometimes my ma kicked him out. But Lover's Day would come and the cold always drove him in."

Old Gam stood up and walked over to the little hearth, shaking her skirts back into place. A small stack of twigs and wood was stacked by it and she threw in a few, not cowing before the flames as they leaped up to lick at the fuel. "Well, one night," she started again, watching the fire as she stood there, her skirt painted orange by the light. "We were all sleeping in the bed together as we were wont to do to keep warm in the cold times. I didn't even hear him. But I saw him standing over me, the light from the coals he dropped on my leg making his face glow like something from the Goddess' hems, eyes wild, mouth wide in a judgmental scream. And then his eyes were wide not with fervor but pain. My mother hadn't thought to put the coals out on my legs but she did kill him. She broke his back with the ax. You don't mess with a woman from the Freewild. I passed out from the pain shortly after. They got me to a priestess in the Valley proper for healing but there was no medicine for him. No moonflowers grew over his grave. Just the fluttering of dark wings, I suppose."

Old Gam came back to the table and sat down. She set her elbows on her knees and laid her head in her hands, gazing at the little girl before her. "So you see, we have something in common. We've had people mistreat us. I doubt you did anything to deserve such a cut, you don't seem very insolent and you seem very fast." Old Gam raised her brows at her. "So… who did it?"

Tavera could feel her mouth dry out and she wished she hadn't drank all of her beer. Her heart thumped in her chest and she traced a skinny finger around the circle she made, wishing she could finish it and wondering when Derk would be back. But Old Gam was staring at her and she had asked and she had shared. Tavera could still imagine the scar on the woman's skin and she couldn't help but feel her own skin crawl and pull tight and itch on her legs. Biting her lip she cleared her throat and forced herself to speak.

"I...when I's with my father's debt holders, they cut it. And they sent it to him. Since he couldn't read. To make him pay. I..." She sucked in her breath and held it for a moment before she spat the last bit out. "I don't think he ever paid. So they sent me to the Blocks." Everyone knew what the Blocks were. Tavera had gotten off easy for a little girl from the 'Wicks. Orchard work, gleaning, fish gutting and finally...sausage making. She still hated sausages to this day. Tavera put her hand up to where her ear was cut and frowned.

"There, there," Old Gam said. She sat up and knelt besides the little girl and she hugged her, letting Tavi bury her face in her neck. Old Gam smelled like milk and sleepspice and Tavera tried to remember what her mother and father had smelled like but could only remember Derk. His skin, the tobacco he smoked, the oil he put in his hair and the iceleaf he chewed sometimes, occasionally mixed with alcohol.

"And don't you think that people like that...they give the rest of us a bad name, don't they? Not every person from the Freewild is like my pa and not every gambler and debt taker is like those people who did

this to you." Old Gam smiled and gave her a kiss on
the cheek. "And if you're good at what you do and as
clever as Derk says you are and you stay sparkling like
you are, you'll get to set things right. And have fun on
the side." Her brown eyes strayed down to Tavera's
lap and she smiled. "Look, you're almost done. I'll
make you a bedtime drink. Derk'll be back soon." She
ruffled her hair with her hand, and it made Tavera
grimace with annoyance which, in turn, made Old
Gam laugh. She went back to the kettle and threw
some herbs in and stirred it with a wooden spoon,
coming back to sit while it steeped.

Tavera finished her circle and she smiled at it, a
crooked little smirk. A circle was harder than a
square, she told herself and she had made a perfect
circle. Tavera had decided she had admired her work
enough and was about to hop out of the chair when
Old Gam spoke up. "Has he ever mentioned a woman
named Sindra?"

Tavera shook her head and looked at Old Gam's
face, trying to figure out what she was looking for.
Derk hadn't mentioned anyone by that name. "I don't
think so," she said finally. "Just you." The little girl's
words made color come to Old Gam's cheeks though
she didn't look up from her work. Tavera stood next
to Old Gam and looked over her shoulder at her
work. It was a handkerchief with daggerleaf crawling
over the edges in a pale green, the red flowers popping at the corners. "Who was she?" she asked, not

sure if she should say the name. Was that the woman she was supposed to look like?

Old Gam just sighed, managing a few more stitches as she did. "Just some woman your pa used to fancy when he was younger. I never met her but she was around, if you catch my meaning." A bit of annoyance showed in Old Gam's face. Apparently she didn't like to be on the receiving end of some questions. Tavera focused on the handkerchief Gam was sewing, surprised to see the progress the woman had made in the short amount of time.

"You're good at this," Tavera said finally. A circle was one thing but a straight line of various shapes was something different altogether. Plus Old Gam didn't sew up and down as Tavera did. Her thread looped around and collected in chains and sometimes the stitches ran next to each other to give the effect of smoothness, filling in little pools of color on the square of cloth.

"I know," Old Gam said, pleasure with the compliment dripping from her words. "I've been doing this a long time. Longer than you." Their eyes met and Tavera took a step back, seeing something hard in Old Gam's eyes she hadn't expected to see. Just as she took the step back a knock came on the door and then Derk popped his head in, his familiar grin setting Tavera's nerves back to normal.

"You ladies doing alright?" Derk asked, stepping in and taking off his cloak. He shook it out before he set it on the peg, running a hand through his hair before he looked at them both, smiling. "What'd I miss? You get to sewing, Tavi?"

Tavera nodded and walked over to him, showing off the circle she had made, trying hard not to grin too hard with pride. He took it up in his hands, the rough skin scratching against the fabric as he held it gingerly, looking at it before he set his eyes on her. "You did this, Tavi? Well, this is just...I didn't know you was a seamstress as well as a cunning little girl! You could sew coins into your clothes this way, d'you know that? This is a very good circle!" He pulled his chair over to Old Gam and sat on it backwards, straddling the seat as he looked at the handkerchief. "And more of the same delicate work, beautiful as always." He took one of Old Gam's hands and kissed her fingers and Tavi saw him bite her knuckles gently, which made Old Gam laugh. "Celeel, you could get a job in a keep, I swear on Her tits. Any Baron would be more than happy to have your work on their tunics and britches. A priestess maybe."

"I started doing work for the priestesses of the temple, actually," Old Gam said in a matter-of-fact way, as she sewed a few more stitches, lowering her eyes at Derk in a way that was supposed to be demure. "Just the every day clothes, though they might want me to do the altar cloth for Lover's Day."

"Really?" Derk's eyes went wide and he looked to Tavera. "Did you hear that? What an honor! Oh, speaking of the temple," Derk said, standing up quickly from the chair, standing upright in one fluid motion, he spun the chair back to its original position with the light touch of his hand, making Tavera giggle with his showmanship. "They was selling these outside the temple and I thought you might like one." He patted his hands against his chest and pulled out a small carved stone, the impression of a lantern carved into it. "You know about the story of the Goddess as the Light Bringer, I trust."

Tavera nodded and looked over the smooth white stone, feeling how cool it was in her hand and how it was warming against her skin. "The…the goddess walked along the night and saw how scared the people was in the dark and how they cried. So she went to her brother, the Sun and asked him for a bit of light for the people in the night, asking for mercy. Her brother said he couldn't, saying they would love him more if they saw him less and turned her away. So in the night she crept to where he kept his flame and she stole it, just a handful which burnt her hands black but she ran with it back to her realm of the night. She lights the night sky for everyone and every month goes back to steal more light for her people, that they might not fear the dark. And sometimes the moon is red because he catches her and they fight and he bloodies her."

"Beautiful. I don't think I've heard a priestess tell the story better," Derk said. He walked over to her and took her by the hand, her hand so small in his and he spun her around to imaginary music, making her dizzy and pulling a laugh out of the little girl. "Tomorrow we'll go by the temple so you can make your offering and yes, before Old Gam insists, you and I will go see someone else for a different sort of blessing." Tavera stood there dizzily and Derk crouched down before her, looking at Old Gam over his shoulder. "He's in Bluemist, isn't he?"

"On personal business is what I heard," Old Gam said. She shook out her skirts and walked over to the fireplace, pulling the pot off the fire with a metal hook and setting it on the small stand. "He'll be happier to have you find him in Tyestown. And there'll be more for the girl to do there."

"Bluemist is pretty though. The mists do look blue as they rise off the lake, I've seen them. If there was a list of prettiest places in the Valley that were actual places, it would be one of them." He walked over to her with the mugs, holding them while she ladled the drink in, steam rising off. "I'd probably add on Northtown for its view of the Holy Bowl."

"The view from the Freewild is better," Gam said, pouring milk into both mugs. "And please, do wait for it to cool before you drink this, you stupid man." He crossed his eyes at her and walked over to Tavera with the mugs, blowing over the top of his as he walked to the table.

"Too bad there's nothing in the Freewild but nameless towns and jackasses too stupid or too miscreant to stay in the Valley proper." Derk set a mug in front of Tavera and she blew across the top of it, smelling the spices and herbs in the drink. "In any case what would you rather see, Tavi? Some blue mist, maybe get some fish stew? Or Tyestown? They have some of the nicest dance halls in the Valley and I do know how you like to move those feet of yours." He kicked her under the table and picked up his mug, taking a sip and screwing up his face as it burned his mouth.

Tavera could only nod enthusiastically, wondering what the dance halls of Tyestown looked like. The 'Wicks had several but their steps were always kept clear of children and people not associated with the establishment. It was a place for merry making and music. The streets around the halls were kept lit and free of drunks and beggars, usually in contrast to the dark dealings done in the basements or attics of the buildings. A Baron's town would probably have a grand dance hall, wouldn't it? And plenty of people selling and buying and trading, plenty of pockets to check out.

"It's getting late Tavera, so best you drink up and get ready for bed," Derk chided, drinking his mug in a few quick gulps. "You'll sleep out here and Gam and I'll be back there." He gestured towards the back room with his chin. Old Gam ducked into the back room and Tavera could hear her going into the trunk again, things moving in the back.

"Can I have some more thread?" Tavera asked, her shyness finally melted away. Derk reached forward to clean her mouth with his hand. Tavi looked to Old Gam and pleaded without words. Old Gam cocked her head to the side and set the quilts she had in her arms on the floor.

"I suppose you may. Glad you're enjoying the sewing." She did in fact look pleased and she went into the back again as Tavera pulled off her boots and socks, untying her skirt so she was in her tunic only, way too long for her and covering her skinny thighs and knobby knees. When Gam came out and saw her legs she laughed, hard. "Derk, you must feed this girl more! Are you going to use her to pick a lock?" Tavera stuck her tongue out at Gam when she wasn't looking, tired of being called skinny but Derk just gave his little girl a look, urging silently for her to put her tongue back in her mouth.

"I take that to mean you'll be feeding us in the morning then?" Derk said. He put his mug in the bowl on the stand and started to undo the buckles of his boots, smiling at Gam. She rolled her eyes at him before she went into the back room, closing the curtain behind her. Derk shook his head and turned his attention to Tavera, pulling his boots off and undoing his belt.

"Don't stay up too late, Tavi, we've a lot to do tomorrow. You can sew on the way to the town. No arguing. We have to go to temple and then find a ride and people like to leave early, you know that." He pulled his shirt over his head and hung it over the chair, pulling his dagger out of his boot and setting his boots under the chair.

"I can sleep in the back of the cart," Tavera reasoned, letting her head fall to the side. Her hands were still on the cloth and needle, Derk shaking his head and arranging the quilts on the floor to make a bed for her.

"What if we don't find a cart? What if we have to walk? Eh?" Derk laid on the pile of quilts to test it, sitting up and switching the one on the bottom for the top. "I'm not going to carry you, I'm not."

"There's no way we'd ever walk all that way!" she exclaimed, rolling her eyes. Derk put his hand on the side of her head and gave her a gentle push, a silly gesture and she just slapped his hand away, laughing. "Besides, I weigh such a bit, just roll me up and put me in your pack. I bet I weigh less than a pair of boots."

"I'm glad you're in good spirits but please, be a good girl and go to bed." He gave her a kiss on the top of her head and stood up, his arms crossed over his bare chest, watching as she crawled into the quilts and wiggled around in them, trying to warm them up. They smelled like herbs, the kind that keep moths out and she pulled the quilts up higher till only the top of her head stuck out, dark hair splayed against a patchwork of green and pink and yellow. "I like when you smile, Tavi," she heard Derk say. "Are you happy?"

She nodded under the blankets and felt him pat her on the head, smiling under the quilts. His footsteps grew quieter but she could feel the creak of the floor as he walked away, the rustling of the curtain that was the makeshift door. Tavera moved the blankets and quilts back, too hot to stay under them for too long. Her good ear perked up as she made out the whispering of adults in the next room, deep and middle toned voices taking turns in the dark. The hearth was glowing in the front room and Tavera could still see. She heard them talk for a long time, a few laughs drifting on the air. The little girl could be patient and she waited until the laughs came a bit closer together. Then the talking stopped altogether though the bed was creaking.

Tavera crept out of her bed and walked to the door, remembering which boards made noise and sidestepped towards her cloak. As soon as she was sure she could reach it she leaned forward, grabbing a hold of the heavy fabric and giving it a quick flick to get it off the peg. The cloak hopped off the peg into Tavera's hands and she took the few steps to get back into her bed quickly, sitting on top of the quilts this time. She cocked an ear towards the bedroom, listening. They were still involved with one another so as long as she was quiet they would probably fall right asleep when they were done. Too excited to sleep and by the light of the hearth, Tavera reached into her boot, pulling out the small blue coin Derk had given her. With quick, skinny fingers she placed the coin against her cloak and began sewing it into the fabric, imagining the circle she would create as she pushed the needle in and out.

Tavera was very tired the next morning. She didn't recall falling asleep but Derk had nudged her awake with his toe and she woke with a start, her sewing and needle still her hand. He didn't chide her but he did raise his eyebrows, blue eyes narrowed in disapproval. She could only smile sheepishly.

Breakfast was porridge and toasted bread with honey on top. Tavera gobbled everything so fast Derk had to tell her to slow down. After they ate they packed their things to leave. Gam gave Derk the daggerleaf handkerchief she had embroidered and she gave Tavera a few loops of colored thread, a needle and some fabric. She gave Derk a kiss on the mouth that he returned and she pinched Tavera which made Tavera stick her tongue out at her to her face and the woman laughed. "Remember our talk, Tavi," she said. Derk kissed her again and they left.

"What did you two talk about?" he asked on their way to the temple. The air felt cold but the aromas of the town waking up wafted from windows and mixed with the scents of the streets. Tavera had the rock he had given her in her hand, still cool on her skin. People were baking bread and she wanted some. Would they get food before they found a cart?

"Didn't you two talk before you went to bed?" she asked, scrunching up her nose. Derk stood up straighter and grabbed the straps of his pack, hopping over a rather questionable puddle and taking Tavi's hand to help her over it.

"Well, a bit but I don't recall all of it. I don't know if you noticed but she generally likes to be the one asking the questions." They walked for a little bit more, turning a corner. Tavera saw the temple at the end of alley, the whitewashed steps inviting them in. Derk cleared his throat. "Is that really who did that to you, Kiff? To your ear?"

Tavera gnawed the inside of her cheek as they walked, not sure what to say. One look at Derk's face and the little girl suddenly felt guilty and she shook her head. "No. I...I lied to Gam." She looked back at Derk and waited to hear what he would say, wondering if she had done the right thing in both cases. At first the man looked confused, but it quickly gave way to relief. He nodded and then skipped over to her side of the alley, putting his arm around her shoulders, giving her a gentle squeeze.

They reached the temple steps, beggars and priestesses standing around while a few of the brass stood on the street level, still selling their wares when people were making the morning bread. Derk nodded his head in greeting to all of them. He held Tavera's hand as they both walked up, squeezing it gently as they crossed the threshold.

Tavera looked at the holy water and dunked her whole hand in, wiping it on her forehead and her heart. Derk dipped his fingers in only, choosing to just touch his fingertips to his forehead and heart as they were supposed to do, giving Tavera another look of admonishment. She sucked on her bottom lip and clutched the stone in her hand.

It was quiet in the temple, several people praying with their hands over their heart. This temple had a statue of the goddess standing in a boat. Most of the temples by the water had the goddess standing in a boat, the gentle crescent shape under her feet, a lantern in the right hand. Some depictions would have her with her left hand empty and held to the side, bidding the worshiper to go their way, unburdened.

Tavera had seen them but never prayed at one. This one, though, held the silver knife, hilt towards the temple, the silver blade laid against her black, holy hand. Some said it was for gutting fish and indeed, little stone fish popped around the wooden boat, ready to submit to the goddess wishes and feed her children. But the Mysteries said the knife was meant as a tool of prayer.

Tavera stared at the knife in the goddess' hand, the hilt towards her and she wondered what she would do if she was given a knife. Would she use it to give someone bad what they deserved? Or would she use the knife the way the priestesses sometimes told the laypeople to use it: to cut the past away. She looked to the side and Derk stood there, his eyes closed. What would Derk do? Did Derk hate anyone? Tavera knew what Old Gam would do. But what did Tavera want? The lantern was meant to light her path and the offering stone was in her hands. Tavera bit her bottom lip and threw the stone towards the boat, the stone landing within with a thunk and a splash of water.

She looked to Derk and smiled. Derk smiled back at her and they left the temple together, quietly slipping out past those praying, nodding to the priestess at the door as they left. A few blocks away were the carts heading out of the town and though Derk didn't find one heading to Tyestown he found one heading in that general direction. He made Tavera wait by the cart while he slipped away for a spell and he returned with a bag of stuffed buns. The first one Tavera bit into was filled with sausage and she gagged, spitting up onto the ground. Derk patted her head and tried to smile for the cart driver, assuring him that she wouldn't do that on the journey. The next bun was tested before he handed it to her and this one was filled with fruit and nuts. They hopped in back of the cart with the barrels of oil and settled in as it lurched forward and started down the road.

Derk laid in the back, setting his head against the pack and putting his hat over his eyes, apparently in-tent on sleeping once again. Blue eyes peered out from under the brim as Tavera looked over her sewing things, her mouth twisting and moving with thought. "You like being with me, right Kiff? You're my girl?"

Tavera smiled and nodded enthusiastically, showing her teeth when she smiled. Derk smiled back, sleepily and let his hat fall over his face. Soon he was snoring. Tavera looked over the fabric and the thread and before she could think about it too much she dropped them all over the side of the cart. The sky was finally blue, the haughty sun shining overhead and lighting the day as it wished. Tavera wouldn't hold it against him. She pulled the playing cards out of Derk's pack and dealt herself a hand of Four Seasons, singing to herself as they bumped along the road.

Chapter 4
Cruel as a Child

The bell in the church tower rang loudly, making Tavera jump and then giggle nervously, looking around to see if anyone had seen her. No one seemed to notice though the sound did change the direction some people were walking in. It was the end of the second watch, when many people went home for midday meal so some of the shops and stalls usually closed. Derk had told her to meet him outside the Three Brothers after third watch for evening meal and a bit of talk. He had a meeting with Hock all day at the Weaver Dance hall and she walked by it five times now in the hopes that he would exit the big wooden building with the shuttles over the doors. The last time she had walked by a man with brown hair and green eyes had shooed her away and told her not to come back. She couldn't go back after that, knowing she had been recognized.

The streets of Tyestown had fun things to see anyway. It was bigger than Portsmouth even, maybe bigger than Eastwick and Southwick together but not as scary. It was cleaner and the Baron had even planted gardens and trees throughout the town, little quiet spaces for the townsfolk to sit and work and play. Even the block lords seemed fancier in this town. Derk had pointed them out. They dressed nicer and hid their weapons better than the ones in the 'Wicks though one of them had a very large dog on a very strong leash. Tavera had been afraid of the big black beast but Derk approached the small company, pulling a piece of sausage pie out of his pack and asked if he could feed it to him. The man with the face full of freckles had laughed uproariously and said to go ahead, the big dog rolling onto its back and looking rather foolish with its fat pink tongue falling out of it's mouth. It had fat black teats and the man with the freckles had a black and white puppy pop its head out of his shirt, whimpering for milk. Tavera had pet both the dog and the puppy before they went on their way.

"Don't beware the dog, beware the owner, Tavi," he had told her as they went their way. "If I had it in for that man I'd be dead right now. A man like that can't afford to have poorly trained dogs. One stupid child and he'd be in the clacks." That had been two days ago, a day after they arrived in Tyestown. The pair arrived several days ahead of Hock and tried to make the most of it, walking the town together and separately, learning who the guards were and where they went at the end of their shifts, trying to pick up on the patterns weaving the tapestry that was Tyestown.

Weaving was the biggest industry here and they had passed through fields dotted with beasts of various coat qualities and colors. The villages around Tyestown dealt with animals and grew the precious plants and animals used to make the dyes which gave their fibers the rich colors coveted by others in the Valley. One of the towns was supposedly a swamp where a certain kind of snake hunted and dwelt, its venom giving the most rich, purple dye the Barons coveted for their own garments.

Tavera was trying to decide what her favorite color was as she walked down the street where merchants had swatches of fabric outside. Thin summer reed linens, thick sheepbush spun for winter garments and even animal skins dyed colors they weren't supposed to be. She saw what was obviously a rabbit skin dyed a funny shade of grey and green hanging from the top of a stall and Tavera wondered if it would look nice with her cloak. But the greenish hue would make it stand out more. White was nice but got dirty quickly. The grey was very pretty and looked so soft, Tavera felt her hands twitch wanting to touch it.

How many rabbits would it take to line the inside of a cloak? Probably more than she could afford. More than she could take. She didn't know how to catch rabbits either. The rabbit furs hung outside her reach, twisting in the slight breeze. Tavera pursed her lips together as she considered what it would take to steal the contents of an entire stall of hides and she squeezed her forearm, feeling the hard little band of muscle there.

Her ear twitched under her hair and she turned around, still squeezing her arm. Down the street came a group of children, talking and whooping. Two of them carried wooden boxes with holes in them, something moving inside. Tavera took one last glance at the rabbit skin she coveted and followed after them, keeping to the side as they walked, one of the boys was swinging a stick around while a little girl played with a doll. It wasn't a fancy doll, just rags but it had a big handful of black wool for its hair and a silly face painted on.

Some of the children were eating and Tavera decided that they weren't from Tyestown. They were dressed too nicely and it wasn't a holiday. They were probably visiting the city for a special purpose, several families traveling together for safety and the children had been brought along for a treat. Their clothes were nice but village nice. If their parents sold everything in their cart the children would probably all receive a treat and maybe a new article of clothing for the next holiday or season, maybe a new pair of soft gloves or boots if it was time. Five children made up the band. Probably cousins and a set of siblings. The little girl had to be related to someone or no one would have let her come along. Tavera was probably of age with the two middle ones. The biggest one offered the other half of his pocket pie to the little girl with the doll and she took it happily, offering a bit to her toy before she took a bite out of it herself.

They settled in one of the grassy squares. The two biggest children were carrying the crates, a boy and a girl. They settled on the grass and opened the doors. From one of the boxes hopped a fat, speckled rabbit, grey and brown. Its nose wiggled. The other rabbit had to be coaxed out by the boy, a light grey bunny with tufted ears. The boy pulled something out of his pocket and the bunny hopped shyly towards his hand, wiggling its nose and then burying its face in his palm, making him laugh. The little girl reached forward to pet the bunny but fell forward awkwardly as it hopped beyond her reach before she could pet it.

Derk had given her money for midday meal, asking her to please pay for her food in Tyestown, at least until after the meeting. The money had been stitched into the hem of her sleeve and she bit at the string with her teeth, pulling out the two blue coins that were more than enough for anything she would want to eat. She wanted to approach the children but she hesitated. Tavera didn't get along with other children very well and the big one did have a stick. What if they made fun of her? What if they pulled her ear? Or called her names? She recalled she had tried to punch a grown man for making fun of her pa, scratching at him with her sharp little nails. Would she defend herself the way she had defended Derk's name? She knew how to hit. And a scrap between children probably wouldn't call the guard's attention, just the parents.

The bunnies were too cute. Tavera frowned, wondering why she was already thinking about fighting these children. She had the money in her hands, ready to buy one of the rabbits from them and she felt her face become hot with embarrassment, her hands both wanting to touch the soft fur of the animals and push through the children. She dropped the coins into her boot, wiggling her foot till they both lay firmly under her heel and she took a deep breath, taking a rather forced step towards the children.

One of the middle children looked up first, smiling at her happily. Tavera could hear them talking, the cadence and accents telling her they were from the country as she thought. The fat rabbit hopped forward and Tavera giggled, putting her hands in front of her mouth. The biggest girl looked to her and smiled, her front teeth making her look a bit like a rabbit herself.

"Hello," the big girl said, friendly enough. She really was a big girl, wearing the wide belt around her middle that women wore, her small breasts already pushing past the soft leather. Her brown hair was plaited into two long braids, each one fastened at the end with carved bone fasteners. The boy had reddish brown hair and a ruddy face, his cheeks making his face teeter somewhere between childhood and adolescence. Tavera wanted to pull at her own hair and wished it was longer. It grew in slow but thick and she wondered if she would ever be able to have fat braids like the big girl.

"Whas your name?" the middle girl asked, scratching the fat bunny on its head. Her hair was a bit curlier than the older girls, and she looked to be of age with Tavera, though Tavi was taller. The middle boy had dark curls and light eyes while the one with the doll had the same reddish brown hair of the older boy, curls piled around her head.

"Kera," Tavera said, kneeling down besides them. "Can I pet your bunny, please?" She held her hand out as she did and the other children moved so she could reach the fat one, her fingers sinking into the fur, giving away how small the rabbit actually was under there. "I like your rabbit," she said.

"Iss name is Burly," The oldest girl said, smiling. The rabbit was so incredibly soft it made Tavera draw in her breath. She wanted to sleep in a pile of rabbits though she knew they could kick hard with their back legs. "I just got me rabby today," the girl said, looking very pleased with the giant grey bulk of hair with ears. "Ee should bring a gripper of lunars, don't yeh think?"

Tavera just nodded, petting the rabbit. All she knew about rabbits were they tasted good and were soft. How hard could it be to keep a rabbit? These children did it. "D'you live close?" Tavera asked. The big boy nodded. His stick was right by his hand and the middle boy took it up, skipping over to a little ledge made with stones and balancing there, carefully putting one foot in front of the other. Tavera could have walked it in her sleep, she thought.

"A ways away, down byern the Lady's Necklace, in Bluegrass. Yeh heard of it?"

Tavera shook her head slowly, watching the boy try to balance on the ledge, almost falling to the hard packed ground but catching himself before he spilled. "Uh…yeah. That's south of here, right?"

"And where yeh from, city girl?" the one that had been balancing asked, spinning on the front of his foot. All of the country folk chuckled except for the littlest, too busy playing with her doll to notice what the big kids were doing.

Tavera almost spat at him but she didn't. The rabbit hopped gently away, sniffing the other rabbit with a bit of interest. "I'm from Portsmouth." She left it at that.

"What're yeh doing here in Tyestown, then? That's a ways to come. You into fiber too?" The big boy picked up his rabbit and held it in his arms, the muscled, tanned arms of a boy who worked out in the fields. Probably herding rabbits. His rabbit seemed to want to dig inside of his shirt, its front paws scratching at his chest.

"No," she said carefully, looking to the two girls who hadn't said anything yet. The middle one who said hello was feeding hay to the fat rabbit, the little one making the doll walk across the grass. "My pa's a singer and he's trying to get work at the dance hall. Everyone knows the dance halls in Tyestown are some of the finest in the Valley." She said it in such a way if they hadn't known it they would feel stupid. "Anyways, what are you? All cousins?"

"Garin there's me cousin, Bee there's me sister," the big boy said, pointing to the balancing boy and then the girl with the doll in turn. "Merika and Kela are cousins. We got to come along to sell the shearings, since we didn't come to town proper for Baron's Day." He put his rabbit back in the case, closing it carefully. "Meri and I's birthdays was two phases ago. We's old enough to join the rest of the adults with the raising and breeding, finally, so she got Burly and I got Twitch." He almost blushed, though there was a bit of pride on his face, behind his red cheeks. Tavera pet the fat rabbit again and decided that he liked Merika. They'd probably grow up seeing each other every day, raising rabbits and take vows and have their own babies who would grow up to talk strange and wear nice clothes just to go to the city.

"Yeh, Ferix is big enoof to be interested in the breedin'," Garin said, smiling slyly at Tavera. He twirled the stick in his hand and Tavera stood up, walking over to him. He spun it in his palm and Tavera's hand shot out, snatching the stick from him.

"Shut up," the big boy said, the girls he was sitting with giggled behind their hands. Tavera didn't care what the big boy wanted or was interested in. He could bed his rabbit for all she cared. She hopped up on the ledge with the stick and held the stick across her shoulders and behind her neck, draping her arms over it as she walked across.

"How much was them rabbits anyway?" she asked. A rabbit could be kept in a little hutch and they ate hay. Hay was easy to get. A live rabbit probably cost less than a dead one. You had to pay for the butcher and the tanner and all that when you got a skin. Maybe a young rabbit that had already been weaned. She could feed it until it got bigger and kill it when it was big enough to suit her needs. It couldn't be too hard to raise one or kill one. It could sleep with her in the meantime, keeping her warm at night.

"We traded a whole year's worth of shearings for these two rabbys," said Merika, the big girl with the rabbit teeth. "These two'll make lots of wool. The first shearings will go into a babe's blanket." She smiled at the little girl with her doll and then at Tavera, her eyes sparkling with hope as her rabbit hopped a few more steps, sniffing at Twitch's box.

A whole year's worth of shearings? Whatever that was, it sounded like a lot and Tavera and Derk didn't have a years worth of anything with them in Tyestown. Tavera turned on her heel and walked down the ledge again, her mouth pulled in several directions as she thought. "How many rabbits do you have?"

"Just these," Ferix said, putting his hand on his rabbit's box, sitting up straight. "Just to start. But soon enough, we'll have grips of them. They grow fast, too. But iss worth it, all the hard work, raising 'em up, keeping 'em safe from wild dogs and burrow-bears."

Tavera dropped one hand from the stick, letting it swing around so that she held it like a sword. Garin reached for it and she snatched it away from him, the stick whistling through the air. She wondered how many rabbits they had. Green fields dotted with small balls of hair floated into her mind, people walking around them with clubs or maybe spears, spreading hay on the ground in the winter...what would she be doing when Ferix and Merika got back to their village? She looked over and saw that Ferix was looking at the girl Meri, who blushed behind her freckles, playing with one of her braids. As much as having rabbit fur to line her clothes made her hands twitch, she didn't feel like getting a crop of rabbits and living in a hut while the fuzzy animals hopped around, their noses twitching, their tails wiggling. They were cute and soft but it seemed very...boring. Plus, what would Derk say? He didn't seem the kind of man to live in a hut surrounded by animals. Maybe it made other people's hearts beat but not her own.

"And what d'you do in the city, eh?" Garin asked, grabbing for the stick again. Tavera let him have it and she walked a few steps away from him, trying to find something else to balance on.

"I go with my pa," she said and shrugged, feeling the two coins move under her foot as she placed one in front of the other, imagining a line in her head to follow. "But sometimes if we find a band, I dance and people pay to watch."

"You don't," Garin said, cocking his head to the side. The temple bell went off in the distance, signaling that midday prayers were over and slowly more people filled the streets, those who hadn't been to temple back from their meals. Tavera laughed, thinking how this was one of the few things she had told them that was the truth and Garin had called her false.

"I do," she said. She spun on her heel and then leaned forward so that her body was parallel to the ground . She put one hand on the ground and shifted her weight, sending her legs over her head and then down to the ground, a one handed somersault that had Kela and Bee clapping their hands.

"That's just a turnover, I can do that," Garin insisted, putting the stick down before he put his left hand on the ground. He moved forward a bit, obviously reconsidering before he put his right hand down instead, trying to vault himself forward but landing clumsily on his side instead. Tavera moved out of the way of his wreckage and laughed, not putting her hands over her mouth when she did. The other girls laughed and Ferix just rolled his eyes at Garin.

"Garin, don't ruin yer good britches, yer pa will whup you when we get back to the inn."

"They're fine, Fex and asides, that wasn't dancing. What kind of dancing d'you do?"

"Any kind I please, and not no barn dancing neither. You probably hop about like rabbits!" Tavera laughed.

"Don't mind Garin, he prolly just likes you," Ferix said, his voice cracking slightly though he was obviously trying to sound wise. Meri put her hand over her mouth and laughed, Kela following suit. Tavera looked over to the boy who was blushing and making a face at the older boy, his hands balled into red and white fists.

"I don't like this stupid wellie-girl," Garin said loudly and to prove it, he turned to Tavera and pushed her. Before she could be moved she put her hands on his face and pushed back at him, his head snapping back and his push failing to shift her. Tavera ducked and the other children got up and started moving towards them, Garin's face red where her fingers had raked his skin. He moved to strike her. Tavera beat him to it and threw her fist across his chin, not bothering to follow it up with another blow.

The other children were upon them and she ducked and skirted away from them, dodging the big girl's grasp as she reached for Tavi. Some of the adults were looking now, a priestess walking towards the group and tripping over one of the rabbit boxes, almost falling onto the fat rabbit. She could hear Garin screaming down the street, her arms pumping at her sides as Tavi ran down an alley, into another alley past a fortune teller and two dogs that were fighting over what was hopefully a cow bone.

No one was yelling anymore except her own thoughts, her heart still stomping in her chest as she slowed down. Her breath came steady but ragged and she sat down on the ground after making sure it wasn't too dirty, biting her lip and trying to calm down. Once her heart stopped thumping her stomach decided to growl, clawing at her insides and she realized she still hadn't had a midday meal. Tavera looked around to be sure no one was looking and fished one of her coins out of her boot, holding it tight in her palm as she followed her nose back towards the food carts, not able to keep herself from peeking around the corner for familiar faces.

Her stomach urged her on and she walked quickly to a cart that was selling coal-cooked meat. She scanned the food square quickly and found another cart selling flat, fluffy bread and she paid for two pieces of bread with half a coin, taking it over for the other man to deposit a strip of juicy, charred meat onto, chunks of green onion dropped on top. She handed him the other half of the coin and ducked back into the alley, cramming the food into her mouth. The green onions were slippery and crunchy, still slightly raw so her tongue tingled after her food was gone.

One of the men from the next watch walked past the entrance to the alley and Tavera stood up, brushing her dress free of crumbs, deciding to see if she could figure out where he lived. She knew he usually watched the northern road leading to the lake and when he headed that way she should leave to try and find Derk. She could kill time and maybe find out something useful.

People were still walking about, getting last minute food items for the evening meal, the farmer carts having more people around them than the food carts. The man she followed bought a handful of greens, a big bone with chunks of red meat still clinging to it and a small bag of grains, already roasted. A few more errands were run: a trip to the temple, a pass by the side window of a bar for a quick cup of thinny and a talk with the woman who ran the window. Tavera realized she was thirsty and thought about getting something to drink herself but the man went on and he hadn't noticed her yet so she put one foot in front of the other and continued.

Down another alley, past a row of stores specializing in goat wool, then a street with vendors selling threads and yarns of various thicknesses and colors for different types of clothing. They went around the edge of town where the animals for auction were held, their characteristics written out in a pictures for those perusing to see. Some of the animals looked sad and Tavera couldn't help but feel pity for the beasts but she took a deep breath thinking better them than her. She kept on, careful not to follow too closely lest the man feel her presence.

He turned down a residential street, little houses packed close together with clothes hanging from windows. The guard stopped in front of one of the doors and pushed it open and out of the doorway tumbled a large black and white dog, its ears and tongue flapping rather stupidly about its head, its tail smacking the man in the leg with loud thumps. The guard laughed and stood up, patting his own chest and the dog responded by standing up on its hind legs, licking the man's face enthusiastically. From the door popped a little boy, his freckled face breaking into a smile as the guard ushered them all indoors, closing the door behind them with a thud.

Tavera frowned. The boy's face and the dog looked familiar. All the freckles. The dog's face and happy demeanor. They both reminded her of the block lord they had run into, the one who had the dog Derk fed. What was a guard doing with someone possibly related to a block lord? Tavera shrugged and walked by the house, careful not to step in anything that had been tossed out in the night. When she walked by the door she could hear the dog barking inside and the man shushing it, the clatter of bony toenails on the floor. She originally planned to watch the guard until she had to meet with Derk but thought better of it. The guard was probably home till the beginning of his shift.

She spent the rest of the watch roaming around, balancing on any ledge that she came across, hopping off of them and running to find the next one. She was balancing on her eighteenth ledge when she felt eyes on her and she saw Garin staring at her from across the square, his arms crossed over his chest. Adults were part of the group now and he looked like he had been cuffed recently. Tavera just leaned forward and did a handstand, walking a few steps on her palms before she let the weight of her legs fall back towards the earth.

As her feet arched she felt the coin loosen and then fall out of her boot, bouncing off her hip and into her skirts as she planted her feet on the ground, the metallic clink singing merrily as it bounced along the ground. Tavera chased after the coin, seeing something out of the corner of her eye. As her hand closed around the coin, Garin stepped on her foot and pulled at her hair. Tavera screamed and took the coin in her other hand once he took his foot off. A low growl rose in her throat as she got her balance and stood up. She pushed him so hard he fell back onto his backside with a bounce, the adults now looking to see where the scream had come from.

"You hem-chawing Forester!" Garin shouted at her from the ground, and Tavera sucked in her breath as she clutched her coin to her chest, feeling all the eyes now on her. Her skin grew hot. She felt a thousand ugly things boil in her stomach and threaten to explode from her mouth. Instead she just turned and ran, fighting back her tears and her anger, not caring who saw if she was running now. She knew she was fast, just a blur of blue and brown and black cutting its way through the streets, light on her feet. She found the steps up into the rooms they were staying in, showing the keeper the token they had been given for their room before he let her up the stairs.

Tavera still had a few moments before she had to meet with Derk and she didn't want to show up a bedraggled mess or wearing the clothes those stupid villagers had seen her in. She put the chair up against the door before she opened her pack, pulling her tunic and top skirt off, laying them across the bed as she looked over the rest of her clothes. Her nose sniffed at her winter leggings, finding them clean and she jumped out of her boots, sending them flying across the room. Leggings, a different colored tunic, a belt, boots. Tavera pulled a cap out and set it on her head before she shoved everything else back in her pack, looking at the cloak that hung on the peg by the door.

It was too hot to wear it right now but it would cool down after sunset and Derk would chide her if she said she was cold. She yanked it down, noting its lack of rabbit fur around the face and put it on before she left the room. The room guard did a double take as she walked by but said nothing as she sauntered down the steps.

Derk was already waiting at a table at the bar and the look on his face made her slow her steps, lowering her head as she came closer. The lines on his forehead were deep and his eyes could have been said to be smoldering if they were any color but that bright blue. If fire could be blue and angry, that was what Derk's eyes looked like. He was already drinking from a rather large mug, no food before him and he set his eyes on Tavi, not seeming to notice her at first. He looked at her again and his eyes went up and down, from boots to brow. "What's all this?" he asked when she was close enough to not have to shout for her to hear. "You look like a boy."

"But I'm a girl," Tavera said, slumping into the chair diagonal from him. The hat even covered her ears and she wouldn't have to worry about sitting properly, which Derk insisted. Derk just snorted and took a sip of his beer, pushing it towards her before he eyed her again, his mouth seeming to disappear from his face as he pressed his lips together.

"Did you have a nice time on the town?" he asked. He said it like he meant to say it like he cared but he just sounded annoyed. Tavera shrugged, laying her chin on the tabletop. She wrapped her hand around the mug and looked up at Derk, her thin brows furrowing on her small face.

"What's wrong?" she asked. "Your meetings go bad?"

Derk ran his hands through his hair, pulling at it as he blew out his cheeks. "Not bad, just…you remember that man I told you about? Hock?" He waited for her to nod before he continued but before he could he looked up, a forced smile poking the corners of his mouth and making his eyes bigger. He waved his hand over his head and Tavera turned in her chair to see who he was waving at.

The man he was waving at couldn't be a thief. This man was too fat. He was having trouble getting through the rows and aisles of chairs. He had a great brown mustache sitting under his lip and framing the sides of his mouth. His large frame bumped into chairs and patrons as he made his way to the table and he sat down next to Tavera, the little girl unable to keep from staring at him as he settled in. Hock drummed his fat fingers on the tabletop and looked to Derk first, then Tavera, raising a brow at her. "And who's this lad? Are you starting to collect children, Derk? Start a bench school for little takers?"

"This is her, Hock, this is Kiff," Derk said. Tavera could hear the hint of exasperation in his voice and saw him cover his mouth with his hand in a further attempt to hide his annoyance. It either worked on the big man or the big man didn't care what Derk felt at the moment. Hock chuckled and looked to Tavera. She couldn't help but lean back in her chair away from him, his presence pushing against her. "She's just dressed as a boy for some reason." Derk shrugged and collected his mug back from Tavera, taking another gulp before he gestured towards her with the mug. "Well, here she is."

"A pair of plow-all-days, a pitcher of the bitter and a bowl of yesterdays," Hock shouted at the man behind the counter, making Tavera jump in her seat. He looked to Tavera and smiled genuinely at her. "Would you like something sweet, little Kiff?"

Tavera looked to Derk with big eyes and he nodded slightly. She scratched her cheek with her shoulder and nodded to Hock, feeling a bit shy next to the big man with the loud voice. A man was playing the two-pipes in the corner while a girl sang, both of them not nearly loud enough to drown the man out as he shouted again. "And a bowl of bleeding hearts for my little friend!" He smiled at Tavera once more, pulling a deck of cards out from his shirt and shuffling them with his fat fingers. "Play a game of Woo with me, boy? For old time's sake?" He started to deal before Derk could even nod.

Tavera sat there in her chair, watching as Derk picked up his cards. He didn't bother arranging them, as always, while Hock moved his cards around a bit, trying to get the combinations set up. Hock already had a mate in his hand but not the right combinations to win. The cards were worn but painted by a skilled hand, probably a deck the fat man had bought somewhere. She watched as Derk picked up a card and placed it to the far left in his hand, throwing down a number. His blue eyes didn't scan Hock but Tavera, trying to pick up what she knew about the fat man's hand. She narrowed her eyes as if she were concentrating to let him know Hock had a mate already and Derk pressed his lips together as he stared at his cards, considering his approach.

"So, you like being with this boy here?" Hock asked, picking up an animal card and throwing down a stone card. He didn't look at her when he asked but she still just nodded, knowing he'd see out of the corner of his eye. "And what do you like about being with him?"

"Well…he keeps me safe. And he teaches me. How to tell how much someone has. Where they're hiding it. The best way to turn one thing into another thing. How to plan and wait. And how to fight." She thought back to the fight earlier with the village boy and how it turned out. Tavera fought him back and ran. That was what she was supposed to do. Get away. She had accomplished that though a part of her worried one of the adults in the group would come into the bar and recognize her. The costume change might help her avoid detection and if they were looking for an adult similar in appearance to her no one looked less like her than Derk.

"And what does he get out of it, little one?" he asked, watching as Derk picked up the card Hock threw down, exchanging it for the fire card he had in his hand. Derk's eyes shot over to Tavera and for a second she though she saw alarm there. Tavera felt confused. What did Derk get out of what? Out of Tavera being his daughter? She frowned, taking the mug and pulling a sip off of it, swishing it in her mouth, the beer fizzing and tickling.

"I guess he gets help. I'm a good helper. I'm small and I fit into places he can't." Was this the kind of answer he was looking for? Tavera's mouth dropped as she tried to give a good answer. "And two crows see more than one, right?"

"True, two crows see more than one. So, you're a good helper. But are you a good taker?" He looked over at her now and he didn't look as kind as he had before. Tavera was starting to dislike him. A man set a dish with two roasted rabbits, a pitcher of ale and a bowl of chopped bloodroot and barley salad on the table, setting a bowl of heartberries in their juice before her. She didn't bother asking but ripped into one of the rabbits, thinking of the two she had seen earlier today. This one wasn't soft at all. Just crispy on the outside and juicy on the inside. If she saw Garin again, maybe she'd bite him.

"I'm a good taker," she said, mouth half full of meat. "I took stuff before I met my pa and not just food. And I'm a good watcher, too. Derk says I barely needed teaching on that."

"Oh, and what have you watched as of late? You seen anything of interest?" Hock threw down a rain card and picked up another flower, Tavera seeing the man's displeasure with his cards. Derk looked to her but she kept her face still, dipping a bit of meat into the berry juice, painting it pink.

"I saw that one of them town guards is helping the block lord with all the freckles," she said quietly. "The one with the big black dog. He's got some boy of his living in one of the small houses by the animal blocks. I saw it today while you all were having your meetings." Tavera didn't care if she sounded a bit insolent. She didn't like the way Hock was talking about her pa. She wanted to ask him what was the last thing he stole but it would probably upset Derk. Tavi hadn't seen Derk like this before. As angry as she was, she still didn't want to ruin anything Derk had going with this man who seemed to be important.

"So, you get training and he gets a lookout. That's good. For now." He put down a card and picked up a good one, a leaf card, before he reached over Tavera and lifted a haunch of the rabbit off the plate, ripping into it with his teeth. Derk hadn't eaten anything but was trying to stare at his cards, looking to Tavi for a clue. She wiped her nose with her hand, though she shouldn't have. Derk put down another leaf card, picking up a card from the pool and taking a gulp of beer. Hock smiled.

"Though the bit about the dog and the boy, that's

good to know. You're not bad to have around. Of course, him having you around and us keeping you for ourselves, those are two different things. D'you understand that?" He looked to Tavera, his brown eyes serious in his pale face. His hair showed a bit of grey as he looked at her, the lantern light illuminating the age in his face. Hock looked her over and laughed, setting his cards down on the table. He picked up the leaf card and put it on top of his pile, picking one he didn't want and setting it out, flipping all his cards over for Derk to see, grinning. "That was a quick game now, wasn't it?"

Derk gave her a look that was half a glare and half a smirk, throwing his cards on the table while Hock laughed. "She knows when to pick sides now, at least!" Hock almost shouted, laughing again before he took another huge bite out of his food. "Going for the big win, were yah?"

"As always," Derk chuckled, collecting the cards up and putting them in a pile. Hock finished the bit of rabbit with a loud, slurping sound and set the mangled bones on the plate, wiping his hands on a piece of cloth that had been dropped there as well.

"Well, I've met the girl and had my say. Where're you headed to next?" Hock asked, collecting his cards in his large hands. Tavera ate one of her berries, wondering what Derk would say.

Derk just shrugged. "Probably north, not sure yet. I've been a bit busy with other things to really put an ear in," he said. He looked at Tavera, not with blame but she knew it was because of her. She wasn't sure how she was supposed to feel so she just ate more.

"Well keep an ear in, Derk. We'll be calling on you soon. And maybe we'll call upon your little girl-boy here." Hock heaved himself out of the chair, putting his cards in his belt before he smiled at Derk, a real smile. "Always a pleasure, Derk. Behave yourself."

Derk just nodded and kept his eyes on the table, Hock nodding a goodbye to Tavera before he ambled away, shouting a farewell to the barkeep. Tavera took a spoonful of the barley and bloodroot in her hand, pushing it into her mouth and licking her fingers as she chewed. "What'd he mean, behave?"

"It's something all fathers say to their children," Derk said, shaking his head at her. He leaned over and cleaned her mouth with the cloth, rolling his eyes at her messiness.

"You don't say it to me," she said after she swallowed. She reached to pour another mug of ale but Derk's arm was longer and he did it for her, pushing the mug away from him.

"I do, though not like that," he said. Derk set his arms on the table and stared across the food, not touching any of it. "What did you think of Hock?"

Tavera took another swallow and burped into her hand before she shrugged. "Fat. Kind of nice. Kind of mean. I...don't think he likes me." That wasn't it, not totally. Hock was important to Derk, she knew that. He had taught Derk about being a thief, initiated him into the Cup all those turns ago and he had come to see what she could do. He smiled at her and bought her berries. And he appreciated her helping him with the card game, she knew that. Had she done something wrong? Were her chances at getting into the Cup and making Derk proud ruined?

"It's not that he doesn't like you, it's not that at all," Derk assured her. "He just…you're young. There's only so much you can do and understand. He's more upset with me," he said finally, and it sounded like an admission. "When Hock took me on, it was different. I was older, already a bit known."

"Does anybody want me to be around?" Tavera asked, suddenly feeling angry. Her hands were clenched into fists and she didn't feel like crying. She wanted to hit something. Hock maybe, or Old Gam or Derk, depending on how he answered. Derk sat back in his chair, startled by her question.

"Of course, Kiff. I don't throw girls in sacks once a phase to build muscle, girl."

"I'm not a girl or a boy and I'm not…just your crow, or a watcher or nothing like that," she said. "I'm…I'm Tavera." She was frowning now and her heart was pumping harder than when she had run from the village boy, though all she had been doing was talking quietly. She wondered why she felt so hot all of a sudden.

"I know, Tavi, I know," he said quietly, real names usually reserved for behind closed doors. He got up from his chair and sat beside her, hugging her shoulders. When he did she noticed she had been shaking and when he offered the mug of beer to her she took it, gulping from it noisily. "You still want to stick by me? Even when others think it's a bad idea? I'm sure some family here would be happy to have another daughter, especially a smart one, Though you'll have to change your britches."

Tavera smacked him, wrinkling her nose at him and laughing. He had asked the question but when she looked at him she knew what he wanted her to say. She thought about the people in the town and the villagers and their lives and shook her head. Tavera's ear perked up as the flute player and the singer started up again, several patrons walking over to the small dance floor they had set up. "Pa, what was you like as a little boy?"

Derk puffed out his cheeks and blew out his breath, seeming to search for an answer he could give. "Well blond, for one." Tavera sighed with exasperation and tried to smack him again but he grabbed her hand before she could, pushing it away. "Like most children, I guess. And much like myself today. I looked for adventure and disobeyed my pa. Liked to climb trees, hide from people. Liked girls a lot." He smiled down at her before he pushed her hat back, kissing her on the forehead. Derk stood up from his seat and held his hand out towards her. "Now, the hour of eating has passed, my good sir. May I have a dance or am I going to have to take it from you?"

Tavera laughed and stood on her chair, taking Derk's hand and jumping off the chair. They both walked to the small dance floor, Derk taking her hands in his and leading her in a lively four-step. Tavera rolled her eyes as the singer began to sing. The song was about rabbits. Tavera danced anyway, stepping and hopping to the beat and laughing uproariously when Derk grabbed her by the hands and spun her around till the room turned into one big happy blur.

Chapter 5
Misconceptions & Miscommunications

"By Her paps, girl, what in the hems are you doing?" Derk placed a hand over his eyes and entered the room, closing the door firmly behind him. Tavera stopped mid motion, looking over her shoulder at her pa, then to the onion in her hand, her face void of shame but instead painted with the annoyance of most adolescents. She took a deep breath and resumed what she was doing, not caring if Derk was in the room or not.

"What's it look like I'm doing?" she asked. "I'm rubbing an onion on my tits to make 'em grow bigger."

Derk half succeeded in stifling a laugh, almost

dropping the cigarette he was starting to roll. He finally didn't bother to hold back but instead let out a highly amused guffaw, crossing the small room they were sharing as he did. "You mean to say to make 'em grow at all," he chuckled, avoiding the evil look that Tavera gave him. Her pa laid on the bed and brought the end of the cigarette to his mouth, not bothering to light it but letting it dangle there as he spoke to her, a look of contentment on his face.

Tavera had grown quite a bit since he had taken her under his wing. Her limbs which had once been gangly and too long for her body were now better proportioned and muscled lightly. Her mouth had lost its pathetic drooping and now was pert and full, more apt to be quick with a quip or joke than a sigh or a whimper. Derk had told her she'd be beautiful in a few more years, though more than likely she would lack in the womanly endowments she so desperately wanted. Tavera was doing everything in her limited power to prove him wrong and she continued to rub the onion on her chest, turning her bare back towards him. "That's as big a load of shit I've ever heard," he offered her at last, and she could see his blond eyebrows raising on his face in her head. "Who told you that?"

"Old Gam did, last time I seen her," she said, her voice rich with false wisdom. The sound of Derk's laughter made her purse her lips in anger and her face grew hot with annoyance at him.

"Old Gam? I've seen what she's got 'tween her neck and belly and I wouldn't put any stock in what she's got to say." Tavera heard him try not to laugh and she slammed the onion onto the table and hurriedly pulled her blouse back in, fumbling with the ties as she knotted them. She could see he was trying to take her concern seriously but the smile threatening the corners of his mouth just made her angrier. Derk sighed, loudly. "Besides, why're you so keen on growing before your meant to? You're still young, I think, you've time enough."

Tavera didn't say anything but kept her back to him, staring at the wall. She could feel his eyes set on her and all the humor draining from his voice "What, is there some boy you're looking after?"

Tavera whipped around, her short, dark hair flying and the look on her face betraying her, although she was already protesting loudly. Derk shook his head and made an exasperated sound, looking around the room for something to light his smoke with. "No, no, no, no, no. I don't want you running round with boys or doing stupid things just so they like you. It'll end badly, take my word."

"Take your word?" she half shouted, her voice squeaking as she did. "I ain't never seen you with any women ever, save ma and Old Gam. What d'you know 'bout relations?"

"Relations?" Her father found a match in a pocket of his pack an struck it on the table, lighting the lamp first and then his cigarette. Derk took a deep drag, holding the acrid smoke in his lungs as he spoke to Tavera. "This ain't about relations, this is about young people acting foolish and getting into shit they shouldn't be." He exhaled quickly, almost choking on the last bit of smoke and pointed a finger at her, ignoring the face she made at him. "You start liftin' yer skirts for boys who like big tits, you'll get into the kind of trouble I won't be able to help you with. You'll wind up like Daffy Helk."

Tavera blinked and leaned back a bit. She didn't understand what her father was implying. "What d'ya mean? He's crazy 'cause he's old. That's what the priestess said."

"She just said that because she thought you was too little to know," he said taking another drag, laying back in the bed once more. "But obviously, the truth would serve better in this case. He's like that because he's plowed too many women."

Was he telling the truth? Tavera kept her dark eyes narrowed, her arms crossed over her flat chest as she looked over her father's face, trying to read him. Sometimes he did just say things in jest to her but this time he looked sincere, his blue eyes shining with earnestness. Tavera thought about the old man who wandered the town of Greenmire. He was disgusting and seemed to be wasting away, sores on his fingers and face a clear sign that he was to be avoided. Helk was always mumbling to himself and falling over things, the people in the alleys he frequented staying away from him. How could that be caused by women? She shook her head no. "You're just saying that to scare me."

"I ain't lying. Everybody knows when you sleep with too many people, you give away too much of yerself and you fall apart. His brain ain't right because he's got too many women in there and not enough of him to keep himself together."

"That don't make no sense," she said. "Why don't faithful folk go mad then? Wouldn't they be giving themselves too?"

"They give themselves to the same person though, so themselves is already there. They're just changing it back and forth and coming home to it every night."

"What are they giving?" she asked, her voice more filled with curiosity than disbelief. Derk took another drag, his face tranquil and looking rather pleased with himself.

"Their humors, their personality, themselves. Why d'yah think children look and act like their parents? Even if they've never been around them, they always act like them, or at least one of them."

"Why ain't the brass crazy, then? They sleep with men all the time and most of them have more sense than most." At this, she saw Derk stiffen, sitting up in his chair more; whenever she mentioned prostitutes he behaved this way, growing graver and always speaking poorly of their profession and behaviors.

"They don't give themselves to anyone," he said quickly, flicking the cigarette with such agitation, the bit holding the flame popped out, rolling across the table with its menacing glow. He reached over for the pitcher, pouring more than enough water on it to put it out, the excess dripping off the table and onto the floor. "They don't put any emotions into it, only desire for gain. But I've seen men driven mad by them."

"Well, maybe I can do the same," she shot, flouncing her way to her pack, kneeling down to look for the long, blue ribbon Derk had bought her for her hair. She tied it carefully, feeling the top of her head to be sure it was in the right place. "Maybe you got me too late and I'm like them after all."

He laughed out loud and Tavera cringed inwardly. She heard the melancholy in his laugh and finally she felt ashamed, having made her father think on something sad and maybe causing him grief with his words. She walked over to Derk and sat on his lap, wrapping her arms around his neck and laying her smooth cheek on his rough one.

"You're like me, Tavi," he said finally, kissing her on the forehead like he always did. "You feel things, though you hide it well. You must mind your humors or they may lead you astray. They're good things to have, as they make life richer but you must temper them with prudence. Do you understand?"

"It's bad enough when you're all serious, now you go using big words and such. I hate it!" She grinned at him, her dark face filled with light. Derk's eyes lit up and he stood up quickly, pushing her off of him.

"Tits, Kiff, you sidetracked me so, I forgot. Shamsee's outside, a block towards the temple and needing you for a take. By Her ivory tits, seeing you and that onion made me forget! Go to it, now, it's the one on the left!"

Tavera ran out the door of the room and down the hall, making it to the stairs and jetting down into the tavern proper. The tender raised an eyebrow as she zipped past the bar and darted through the door, almost running into two large guards as she did. They paid no mind to the scraggly girl who shot past them into the busy streets outside.

It was crowded on the street but it was easy to find who she was looking for. The tall, hawk-nosed man called Shamsee was right where Derk had said, a block away from the bar, his small table set up on the tiny sidewalk. Tavera breathed a sigh of relief, seeing she wasn't too late for the take. The man shifted his brown eyes towards her ever so briefly before focusing on the crowd and in a loud, nasal voice he began his tirade.

It went as planned. He broke out the walnut cups and the pea, placing the pea under one of them and shifting them as he spoke in his hypnotizing voice, the crowd gathering around for a look and a chance to play. To prove his legitimacy and the game's simplicity he would ask Tavera, a simple child, to play. He would give the cups a few turns, she would say she couldn't play, as she only had a half piece that her father had given her for an offering at the temple. He would entice the girl, telling her she could make a much bigger offering if she played and won. Tavera would pretend to feign disinterest but play the naughty, poor child and take part in the game.

First she would guess incorrectly. This would cause the crowd to feel bad for her so that when Shamsee offered to double her money if she guessed right the second time, the crowd would become endeared to him for having pity on the poor girl. She would then guess correctly, much to her feigned delight and the pleasure of the crowd. Shamsee will have saved the day and presented himself as a man of honor when in reality he was neither a savior nor an honorable person. She would take the coin and get a bit more of the take later in the day, when he had played what he thought was enough or until a disgruntled and taken patron would turn over his table and try to beat the shit out of him. It was an easy way to help someone out and make a bit on the side.

Tavera laughed out loud, rocking back and forth on the old crate she decided to sit on, pointing at the man who staggered towards her. Apparently the game had been taken too far today and a patron decided to appease his embarrassment by punching Shamsee in the face. He had the beginnings of a black eye and was holding up a dirty handkerchief to his bleeding nose, his hat skewed on his head and making him look even more bedraggled than he already was. He sat down next to the girl and plopped a small pouch on her lap.

"Sure I couldn't pay you in dollies and sweets?" he asked, his voice muffled by the injury and the pain. Tavera snorted at him as she tucked the small pouch of coins away, still wondering how someone who had been doing the walnut bit for so long could still not tell when he was about to get his jaw kicked in.

"Chew Her hems," she cursed, cocking her head to the side and looking over his face. It wasn't as bad as it could have been and he was most certainly acting as if it was worse, his mouth twisted in pain and one eye tearing as it swelled before her eyes. "You're gonna have to go to a bleeder for that, Sham. He's gonna put a nice, fat blood worm on your eye for the swelling. Maybe he'll pick one that's starving and the sucker'll pop your eye clean out your white box."

"Do shut up," he said, his face changing colors from a worked over pink to a sickened green, his eyes wincing at her words. "All this and you were late to boot? What's that? I sent that fapper of a pa of yours after you? You too busy puttin' on frocks to keep yer word?"

Tavera turned her head and glared at Shamsee, her one pointed ear twitching slightly under her hair with anger. She hated when the thugs, the common street hustlers called her father that. She had thrown herself at a man twice her size in Westbrook for say-

ing as much and only her father's forbidding kept her
from trying to give Shamsee a black eye to match the
other. "I don't come when you call. I's busy doing
something when he told me and I came when I was
ready."

"Well, it's bogged to keep a partner waiting. Yer
pa knows it and I don't think he'd a left you dodging
'round the room if he knew you were 'spected some-
wheres. If I told him to get you straightaway, I know
he'd a done it." Shamsee paused for a second, his one
good eye narrowing for a moment, a trickle of blood
shining under his nostril as he did. "He caught you
doin' somefin, didn't he?"

Tavera's pride drained from her face as he asked,
her eyes looking to the end of the alley for a split second, wishing something would happen so she could
leave. That was the problem with some of the streets-
men she worked with. Even if they lacked common
sense, they generally weren't idiots. She didn't have to
answer his stupid questions, even if they had worked
together. This subject matter was unrelated.

"Wait a minute," he said, frowning slightly, eying
her once again. "My nose may be busted but I believe
I smell…onions." He reached over as if to pull back
her blouse but Tavera fell back, screaming as she
swung out at him, her closed fist connecting with his
cheek. He grabbed her wrist with his free hand, somehow able to laugh and he pulled her back onto the
crate. "Hold on now," he said, his smile revealing a

few missing teeth and a half decent smile. "I've sisters enough to know what you were doin' and I have to tell yeh, it don't work."

"I don't know what you're talking about," she shot, her arms covering her chest protectively and giving herself away. Shamsee laughed out loud, almost falling off the crate.

"Oh, this is lovely," he said, clapping his hands and slapping his knee, finally straightening his hat on his head. "I can't believe people still believe that it works. I've got no less than four flat chested sisters prove it don't."

Tavera pressed her lips together, feeling a little embarrassed but somehow less so, knowing that multiple women before her had also tried the fruitless remedy. "Well," she said, hopping off the crate and holding the purse up, the coins jingling merrily. If she changed the subject and left, maybe she could still save face. "Thanks for the work. I'll maybe see you later."

"Hold up," he said, hopping off the crate and walking towards her. "Donchu want to know how you can get 'em to grow?"

Tavera stopped in her tracks. She tried not to care, she really did, but she spun around faster than she knew she should, walking back to the beaten man. "You better not be tellin' me lies, Shamsee."

"Honest to the goddess, and I've proof as well. Listen to me Kiff, the way to get yer tits to grow is by... touching."

"Oh, well that's just lying and you swore!" she said, pushing him with her hands and only managing to move him an inch. He shook his head and swatted her hands away.

"It's true, touching 'em makes 'em bigger. And I ain't talkin' 'bout touchin' em yerself. I'm talkin' 'bout havin' other folks touchin' em. Think on this, what types of womens got the biggest ones?"

Tavera thought about this. The woman she knew with the biggest breasts had been Prisca; they had been large and milky white because she kept them covered when the sun was out. When Tavera had been living with her, she tried to pick one up and had needed both hands to do so. The other woman was a mother with five children, all of them young and still nursing for food. What was he getting at?

"Mams and the brass, I suppose," she offered, trying to guess what his logic was. He nodded, blowing his nose and looking into the grimy handkerchief, grimacing as he did.

"Aye, and who gets their goods touched more than those ladies? Brass by their men and mothers by their children, day and night."

"What're you telling me to do, that I should go out and have people touching me so as to make 'em grow?" she asked incredulously. Even if what he said was true, she didn't see how the plan could be carried out, especially because her father had just said she should stay away from men. It seemed ridiculous and like she would be flat chested all her life.

"I ain't tellin' you to do nuffin," he said, sitting back on the crate. "As an observer, a brother and a man who has actually had quite a few tits in hand, I'm just offerin' a bit of knowledge. You're prolly too young fer men anyways."

"Too young? I'm prolly 13, I'll have you know!" She turned her chin up at him, her fists resting where her hips should have been. Shamsee put up both hands in mock supplication. It made her mad and so she punched him anyway, a sharp, tight blow that made him wince and rub his shoulder as he frowned at her.

"The ripe age of 13? Pardon me, I ain't used to yer kind, little Miss One Ear. You're lucky your pa is who he is, I bet I could make a bit, selling you to someone who wants to be around your kind. Also, well, I don't really dislike you. And I don't know where to find any of those people." He narrowed his eyes at her and the look she gave him made him take a half step back. "Anyways, I'm sure yer pa is waitin' on you back at the Silver. You was a big help to me today, though Kiff...wouldja be willin' to have another go? As a fave? I did give you some good advice, after all?"

Tavera narrowed her eyes. Shamsee was a bit of an idiot and not completely trustworthy but this was more due to his lack of common sense, not actual malice. She could make a few coins for just a few minutes work. And as much as she didn't want to believe what he had said about touching, it did make a bit of sense. If what Derk wished for her happened, she would never have the bosom she hoped for. Tavera shrugged, nodding soon after.

"Fine, yeah…you know where I am. Though you call my pa names again, and I'll make you regret it." And with that, she turned around, her skirts swishing, her straight frame disappearing around the corner, not bothering to look back at Shamsee once as she left the alley.

Touching…she thought about what Shamsee said the whole way back. Could it be true? Why would he lie to her about this? And though Shamsee wasn't smart as thieves come, she did see him around women frequently. Derk hadn't offered any help, just made her feel stupid and gotten on her about boys. Boys. She didn't even really like this particular one that much anyway. Tavera had seen him carrying something in a basket into a shop and thought he was handsome, though not as handsome as her pa. He had curly hair and freckles and apparently liked girls with big tits, since after his shift all he did was stand around some bosomy girl and talk about stuff that made them put their hands over their mouths and laugh. She couldn't make out what he was saying, but she could see him staring at the girl's chest when he thought she wasn't looking.

It wasn't fair. Why did some girls get to be pretty and have big tits while others looked strange and were flat chested and had over-protective fathers? She sighed and let herself into the room where Derk was laying on the bed once more.

"How'd it go?" he asked warmly, sitting up in the bed. Tavera shrugged and pulled her boots off, climbing into the small bed with her dad, snuggling close to him. He smelled like tobacco and sweat and the oil he used for his skin. It comforted her and she looked down towards the foot of the bed, wiggling her toes.

"Sham called you a fapper and ran the bit too long. But I might run it again with him, just for something to do."

"You didn't hit him, did you?"

"I did, but not for what he called you." They laid there for a moment, her father's body shaking as he chuckled, playing with her short hair.

"I talked to someone I know who's opening a tea mercantile. Said he can use some help, someone with quick hands. Interested?"

Help at a store? If Tavera was helping at a business, it meant they would be staying a while. Her one good ear perked up slightly. "Tea? That bitter shit you try to get me to drink when my nose is plugged up?"

"Language, Tavi," he said, wagging his finger. "Yes, tea. I'm thinking you're getting a bit older and it might be good for us to sit for a bit. Winter'll be here soon. It'd be good to learn something new and there ain't shame in work for pay, long as you do keep doing what you do best. What d'you say?"

If they stayed in town, the boy with the curly hair might notice her. She pretended to think it over for a few seconds and then shrugged, hugging her father. "If you think it's a good idea, it might be nice to stick around for a bit."

"Good then, it's settled. Though I suggest you don't do too many jobs with Sham, he's an idiot."

"Yeah," she said, laughing, rolling out of the bed with a thump. Tavera sighed as she sat down by the window, staring out onto the busy streets that she would get to know better, thinking about what Shamsee the idiot had said. Touching. Maybe she could have a beautiful body, or at least something to fill out her blouse a little. Derk would disapprove if he knew what she wanted, even if it did mean that she could have a bit more happiness. It was too early to go to bed but Derk would nap before supper so he could stay up all night, leaving the next few hours free for the girl. Tavi set her chin on her hand and watched the men and women go by, wondering who they were and if any of the women had ever done something so silly as rub an onion on their chest. Tavera smiled at the thought of seeing the boy again. Maybe he would be willing to test Shamsee's trick with her.

Chapter 6
Trial by Blood

Tavera woke up and grimaced. Her stomach hurt and the feeling of pain creeping through her belly had woken her. It was still early in the morning. The birds that typically sang just as the sun was coming up were sending out their calls. The only other noise was the sound of Derk snoring behind her. His arm was draped around her middle, pinning her down. He seemed as if he was deep in sleep but she knew if she spoke he would wake up. They weren't usually early risers but her stomach did hurt, as if someone was squeezing her guts, twisting them gently and she felt a bit nauseous. The heavy arm pinning her to the ground didn't help and so she wiggled a bit under the blankets, hoping to wake him up before she spoke.

"I don't feel good," she said quietly. The change in his breathing told her he was awake though he didn't move yet. She lay there and waited, feeling the pressure on her side lessen as he gained control of his limbs.

"How d'you mean?" he mumbled. A bird tweeted, closer than before. Tavera looked towards the campfire, or what was left of it and tried to think of how to describe it.

"I dunno," she said, wiggling in her bedroll. "I've a stomach ache."

"What did you eat last night?" he asked. He didn't sound annoyed or angry, just tired. The half-elf girl tried to think of what she had eaten last night and realized it would be easier to think of what she hadn't eaten. She'd been ravenous the last phase, eating everything in sight. Derk had chided her on eating too quickly last night, saying it would give her stomach problems. Maybe that was it.

"Same as you," she said, squirming again as another squeeze pushed in her stomach. "Same as always." Derk sat up and she stayed lying on the bedroll, not wanting to get up in the cold air. But he tickled her on the side and she grimaced and laughed at the same time, slapping his hand away as she did her best to keep the blankets around her. Derk reached over and pulled her eyelids up and then down, feeling where her neck met her head and pressing there with his thumb and middle finger. He placed a hand on her forehead and frowned, his blue eyes still weary with sleep and he shook his head.

"You seem well enough. Go make toilet and see if that doesn't help." Derk kissed her on the forehead before he slumped back towards the ground, eyes fluttering closed as his head disappeared within the blankets. Tavera pouted and got up as slowly as she could. It was cold and she shivered as she unwrapped herself from blankets. Twigs and pebbles pressed into her socked feet as she picked her way around the remainders of the fire, walking far enough away from their small camp for privacy. Little ferns and bushes snapped at her legs as she meandered, looking back over her shoulder to make sure she could see the campsite but that Derk wasn't looking, spinning around to make sure no one else was, either.

Derk had probably passed back out. He only bothered her if he thought she was taking too long and right now, it felt like everything she had eaten last night was about to fall out of her. They had lunch in town, and she had gorged herself on roasted barley soup, as many rolls as Derk would buy her, a piece of roasted ground fowl and all the fish they had brought. A few pilfered fruit satisfied her desire for sweets and Derk humored her with a bag of charred nuts on the way out of town. She finished off the bag before he could think to ask for some. Tavera burped. She wasn't hungry at all now. Food sounded horrible. Fumbling hands pulled down her trousers and she squatted down after she kicked around to make sure no snakes or spiders were hiding anywhere.

The birds still chirped and twittered above and about, a little red breasted bird hopping around just a few paces away. The girl made a face at it when it cocked its head at her and she hissed at it when it flew a few widths closer. She finally put her head down to try and block out the little bird, feeling her stomach pains ache lower. When she looked up the little bird was gone. Her stomach was still cramped but at least some of the pressure was gone. She pulled out the rag she had tucked in her pocket to wipe herself, wrinkling her nose as she did and her mouth falling open when she looked at the scrap of cloth.

Blood.

Was it really blood? The girl cursed under her breath. It was pinkish. If the fabric had been darker, she wouldn't have noticed but there was a pink and red smear on the fabric. She finished wiping and left it there, pulling her pants back up and wiping her palms on her thighs as she walked back towards the campsite. Derk was sitting up on his bedroll now, looking in her direction. His eyes were narrowed, watching her carefully as she walked back, tripping over her own feet but catching herself. He looked her over. "Everything alright?"

Hesitant sounds came out of her mouth and she made a few faces as she looked into the embers of the fire, scratching her head. "I...yeah. I just think...

maybe…it started?" She chewed on the side of her mouth, not sure what else to say. Tavera knew what was happening, she was fairly certain. Prisca had told her about it and Old Gam had mentioned it. Derk just looked at her blankly, strangely alert.

"What started, Tavi? Are you sick?" He coughed into his fist, squinting at her. Tavera put her hands under her stomach and felt tired.

"It's…it's my Red Earth time," she said, quietly. In the early morning stillness it still seemed loud and Derk's eyes went wide as they stared at each other for several breaths. Eventually Derk seemed to snap on it and a paranoid smile came across his face as he scrambled up from his bedroll.

"I've got to boil some water," he said, picking his belt up and buckling it around his waist, grabbing his vest off the pile of things that belonged to him. "This couldn't have come at a better time, with Gam being in town. This is your first, right? Tavi? Tavi? Are you okay?" He grabbed the pot and then set it down again, going into his pack and pulling out a pair of pants. "Tavi, come sit down, dear."

Tavi walked over to where the beds were and sat down watching as he pulled off his pants. He put on the pair he had removed from the pack. "Derk, what are you doing?" she finally asked, slightly exasperated by his sudden increase in activity.

"I'm changing into my good pants so we can tear up my old ones for you," he said, buckling his belt again and having some trouble as he had the kettle in one of his hands. "But I've to get water to boil the rags in. Then we have to go into town to the temple so you can have first rites."

"First rites?!" Tavera squeaked. Her stomach was still tying and unraveling, and she squirmed in her seat, wishing she had something to make the pain go away "Like what? Is it like a holiday?"

"I guess I haven't kept you 'round girls your age, have I? Otherwise you'd know. Hasn't Old Gam told you about this?" Derk put a hand up to stop the both of them from talking, his blond hair still mussed atop his head and his shirt half tucked into his trousers. "Let me get this water. If you're up to it, rip these old things into strips. I needed a new pair anyway." He fumbled around in his bedroll, pulling out his dagger and handing it to her. "You'll be alright?"

"It's blood, not brain," Tavera snorted, taking the dagger from him. "What, like for wounds?"

"I don't know!" Derk said and he blushed, avoiding her eyes. "Just think about…what you think you need! But I should boil them first, some of them at least. I'm going!" he shouted, walking away. "Scream if you need me!"

"Fine!" she shouted after him, watching him go. There was a little spring not too far away from where they had set up camp. Tavera ripped off a rectangle of fabric and looked at it, wondering how big it should be. Her gaze wandered towards the fire pit, seeing the pile of sticks that lay close at hand to feed it. She set the pants and dagger aside; Derk couldn't boil water if there wasn't a fire. She stirred the ashes with one of the sticks, seeing if any embers lay underneath. A handful of dried grass fed the remains of the night's fire, going from yellow to brown, then black and glowing orange as they caught on fire. Twigs came next. A low, long yawn was stifled as she heard Derk shout and saw him rush forward, throwing the kettle of water onto the fire she was building.

"What the tits are you doing?!" Tavera started, some of the water splashing up onto her. She glared at Derk, still holding the twigs in her hand. He just looked at her sheepishly, putting the kettle under his arm. "I know how to make a fire, you know it! Why'd you do that!?"

"You can't build a fire-"

"Yes I can, I do it-"

"NOT…now," he said, finally lowering his voice. He rubbed his eye with the palm of his hand and sighed heavily, looking into the empty kettle. "Now… it's not good. You can't build a fire. When you're on your Red Earth time. It's…."

"That don't make no sense," Tavera said and her good ear twitched as she said it. It didn't. Why couldn't she build a fire? She knew how to build one and had done it countless times. Whatever had been left of it was gone now, a pile of soggy ash and grass. "No ladies build fire in their red time? How do they cook then?!"

"It's just…it's one of those things, Tavera," Derk said and when he said it, he sounded unsure about it. "I'm sorry I splashed you. But it's supposed to be… bad. A taboo."

"What like…like plowing children?" She asked it hushed and after she said it, they both looked around worriedly. Derk mumbled something under his breath and set the kettle down, mechanically tugging at the prayer bracelet he wore around his wrist. He shook his head at her, his lips a thin line that cut across his face.

"Not that bad, no," he said, still looking around. "It's an old…like I said. It's bad luck." He picked up the kettle and looked her over again, cocking his head to the side like that bird had done. "You look pale."

"I'm more dark than you."

"Eat something, if you can manage. I'll fetch more water. And do those rags if you can, you'll need them."

"What food is there?"

"Whatever you didn't cram yesterday. I might have something sweet in my pack." Tavera watched him leave and she huffed, blowing her hair out of her face. She wasn't really hungry. Her stomach still hurt, her body trying to squeeze the unused earth out of her, to make space for new earth, new life. That's what she had been taught happened at this time. Prisca mentioned Tavera would start seeing men after her first time came. In all honesty, she hadn't really understood all of what Prisca had said regarding her Red Earth. She would have to start doing what Prisca did and she would get money for it. That had been a long time ago and hadn't come to be. Derk took her in and cared for her whereas Prisca…the sound of Derk's footsteps on the leaves and twigs brought her back to her cramps and her task, ripping a few more rags off of the old pants. The man set the kettle down carefully so as not to spill any of the water and went about rearranging the stones next to the old fire pit, trying to rescue what he could.

"What else can't I do?" she asked, ripping off another strip, using the knife to turn it into two, hand sized rags. Derk shrugged and shuffled over to his pack, picking out the two fire stones wrapped in their special bag. He wrinkled his nose at her as he rolled them out, wiping his forehead with the back of his hand before he crouched into the wind.

"Depends on who you ask," he said, striking a stone against the other. "Some would say you can't drink milk. No kissing babies. I'd say no kissing boys."

"That can't be one of them," she said, ripping of another ring of fabric. The dagger tugged at the seam and she pulled it with a jerk, loosening the piece from the rest. "I know it ain't true."

"You could, I just would prefer you wouldn't," he said, striking the stones again, his back towards her so that his words were muffled. "Or rather, I should say, I wish you would stop kissing boys."

"Oh, pa, you know I only kissed that last one because his mam worked at the Wren! There was a whole bag of seedbarley to get!"

"And just last week it was that red headed one for a bolt of fabric and then before that the dark haired lad with the big ears. I don't even remember what that was about."

"I liked his ears, I thought they were cute."

"Tavi!" Derk said, looking back at her finally. Tavera tried her best to stifle her laugh, making her face long and her eyes big. Her attempt just wiped Derk's stern expression from his face and he sighed, turning back to the fire that he had barely started. "Tavi, just...be careful. If that red headed one and the blond one find out about one another, they could get in a row and then the parents come looking for me."

"Fine, I'll just kiss boys that got no parents."

"That's not what I'm...or what about this?" he offered. The sparks had been transformed into a happy little flame and he grabbed a piece of bigger kindling, snapping it in two before he placed it carefully over the fire. "What about women? You're just hitting men up! That's half the people in the Valley you can't use your tricks on!"

"Some ladies like other ladies, you know that," Tavera chided, forgetting about the rags for the moment. "Don't you remember when we went to-"

"But you shouldn't lie about who you like or want to kiss," Derk finally said. He put another piece of kindling on and got the frame to hang the kettle over, digging its points into the earth. "It's not good to do, to garner ills from thwarted lovers. People don't like to be kissed and left. And besides, I've warned you against being a dog of one use. I don't want you to get lazy."

Tavera kept her thoughts to herself, feeling another cramp twist inside of her making her queasy. She put the torn up pants on her lap and blinked, watching as Derk set the kettle of water over the fire finally. "So…" she said slowly, looking over the dagger in her hand. "We're going to wait for the water to boil, and then boil the fabric and then wait for the rags to dry?"

Derk looked at the water quizzically and then to Tavera. After a breath he shook his head and put his hands up. "You got me," he admitted, feeling around for his pipe. "I ain't done this before, Tavi. I don't know what's going on."

"We're supposed to meet Gam and you wanted to get there by mid-meal," Tavera said.

"I know, I know," he muttered, fumbling around inside his pack. Tavera yawned and laid back on both of the bedrolls. Her father nudged her out of the way, finding the pipe but lacking the tobacco. "Just…."

"Hang them over the fire when they're done," Tavera said, curling up into a ball. Her stomach didn't feel well. Derk looked to her and his eyes softened, sighing as he put a hand on her cheek. A rough hand brushed her hair out of her face.

"I'll take care of it, Tavi dear." He leaned over and kissed her on the cheek, which made her smack at him. He growled at her and laughed. "You just rest and I'll do these up as quick as I can. They're small, they should dry fast. I'm sure we can find something else for you in town to help. Gam'll have something for sure." Derk looked into the kettle and started to pack his pipe, smirking at his daughter. "One good thing about this, most girls start growing in the shirt after they start their red times. Sure you're not crying about that."

Tavera nodded and rolled over onto her side, feeling tired but the sensations in her body and the slight excitement kept her eyes from closing. If it was any other day they would probably still be asleep, waking up when the sun had warmed everything it touched and eating on the road. She was supposed to be practicing her fighting but the girl didn't think she'd be up to it today. Tavera rolled over again so she could see Derk, smoking peacefully on his pipe, sitting by the fire and watching her. "Can I get some tea in town?" she asked. "We used to sell a lot of purple cup to ladies on their Red Earth time. It's supposed to help."

"Whatever you want," Derk said. He peeked into the fire again and they sat there, waiting for the water to boil. Tavera rolled over again and stared off into space, watching the little birds hop and flit about. Every time she thought she could nod off, a cramp would roll through her stomach and wake her up. She finally gave up altogether and sat up and started mending clothes with Derk, being sure to jokingly ask him if it was okay to do so. He made a face at her and they quietly mended clothes as they waited for the water to boil.

The wine was sweet and spiced. Tavera didn't really like it but she was supposed to drink the whole bowl of it. Old Gam smiled at her and brushed her hair out of her face, hazel eyes sparkling at the girl who was now a woman. "How is it?" Old Gam asked, her curly hair framing her round face. They were standing at the altar after vespers. All the other worshipers had departed for drinks or home and the two of them had lagged behind for Tavera to receive first rites. The priestess poured the bowl of wine and gave it to Tavera, saying a prayer over the girl and anointing her with water from the sacred chalice.

Tavera always wanted the temple's chalice for herself but she knew such a wish was bordering on blasphemy. She had mentioned it once to Derk and all joviality had drained from his face, and she had spent all of their meal apologizing. She still wanted them, one of them. This one was made out of some white stone, probably alabaster, and it had been carved to be perfectly round and smooth, the phases of the moon and inscriptions raised on the luxurious surface. Different temples had different styles of bowls and chalices, all of them beautiful.

Most households had plainer ones set in the house somewhere. Gam's was set over her door, for protection. The priestess waited as Tavi drank from the bowl, her grey eyes smiling as she gazed down at the newest woman of the Valley. The wine was thick on Tavera's tongue, warm on the back of her throat and hot in her belly, snaking around where there was a slight ache. What she really wanted to do was sleep but Old Gam had insisted on prying Tavera away from Derk, shooing him away to see Jezlen and taking her out for food and gifts.

Tavera finally drained the bowl and she could swear some of it had made its way to her head. Her brain felt as if it were swimming in her skull and she swayed slightly on her feet, holding the bowl out for Old Gam to take. The priestess smiled with her mouth though her words were serene as ever, like cool water in summer. "Now you have imbibed the Wine of the Beloved Woman. May the desire that grows in you now lead you to happiness. May you grow in strength, wisdom and beauty so you may be a help to yourself and those that may call upon you. May the Goddess shine upon you always, Her glory illuminating your successes and comforting you in your troubles. May you wield your womanhood with the pride and power that it deserves." The priestess anointed her again, splashing the holy water onto the girl before she nodded to Gam and soundlessly took her leave of them, Old Gam saying her thanks before they both turned and left, their footsteps echoing in the empty temple.

Tavera looked down at the bracelet Gam had given her to wear; it was a cord of three strands, red, white and black with a goddess bead threaded and knotted at the middle. Gam hugged her around the shoulders as they walked, and Tavera didn't think it would be right to push her away so she didn't. "Well, women's work has been done," Gam laughed, continuing down the emptying street. Tavera kept up with her easily enough though she was still a bit shorter than the curly haired woman who was Derk's closest female friend. She helped Tavera get situated with the rags so the girl didn't feel like she had a load of laundry in her britches.

Gam wasn't so much a mother figure as an aunt figure, though in this case her pa slept with her aunt whenever they could. Tavera liked Gam well enough and looked forward to the times they crossed paths but she was always glad to have her pa back to herself when they parted ways. Tavera was still young but she felt Gam was jealous of Tavera for some reason and she could never figure out why. Tonight, however, Old Gam was all smiles and happiness. "You've any questions for me, Kiff? Anything you want to know? Derk don't know about this kind of thing after all."

The girl chewed the side of her mouth and shrugged. She could hear music playing inside of the taverns and some children were playing a game of kick-the-ball farther down the street. If it had been any other night she probably would have joined them but not now. Her stomach didn't hurt as much but the pain had tired her out and she wanted to lie in bed. "I guess...am I going to be tired all the time this happens? I don't really like it."

"Oh, no one does," Old Gam laughed, showing where a tooth was missing. She had a pretty laugh, though it was a little brash. Gam turned a corner and Tavera followed, waiting to hear the answer. "Everyone's different is the truth of it. You might be tired now, you might be tired before it comes or a phase after. Every woman is different."

"I know, and every woman is as aspect of the goddess," Tavi said, trying not to sound too exasperated. She normally enjoyed going to temple and hearing the teachings of the priestess and hearing about the attributes of the Blessed Mother. That had been before she was supposed to be like the goddess. Was every woman like the goddess? Some of the women she had known in her childhood came to mind and she tried to push those thoughts away and what they might have meant. Tavera hopped off of the curb, puzzling over something the priestess had talked about. "What was all the 'desire' talk? I don't understand that part. What does having blood pour out of my twixt have to do with wanting?"

Old Gam laughed again and Tavera thought this time, maybe, the older woman thought her a bit silly.

Maybe it had been a silly question but she wanted to know. Old Gam turned another corner, looking around it before she motioned for Tavera to follow, this street quieter than the last.

"It has to do with wanting to bed," Old Gam explained. The sound of something squeaking ran across their path but neither one of them seemed to care and continued walking. Spring clouds loomed up ahead, darkening the sky and hinting at rain to come. "Once your Red Earth comes, you start wanting to bed men."

"But I already like men, or boys at least," Tavera said. She hopped over a crate, standing there for a breath before she strode after Gam, seeing the smirk on the woman's mouth. "I do, Derk's always getting on me about it, saying I shouldn't be hanging 'round boys like I do."

"He does, does he?" Old Gam's voice was dry and she put her hands behind her back, casting Tavera a sideways glance. "I am both shocked and not shocked, Kiffer. He's your man, of course he says that. Tell me, girl, what kind of boys do you like?"

"Oh, usually ones that have nice things, or if their mams are bakers." Now Old Gam laughed loud, so loud that someone threw something at them and they had to run down the street to escape, the both of them laughing and yelling back by the time they got to the door. Tavera had tears in her eyes and Gam was holding her stomach as their laughs settled down to chuckles and then sighs.

"That ain't what I mean, love," Gam said, a grin plastered on her round, amused face. "Not for things, though there is that. I mean desire, wanting like… wanting to tell someone about you, wanting them to know you, all of it. Wanting them to love it, to grab it and press it against them hard, till it melts like snow in the sun. Or even just…." Old Gam's eyes were somewhere else but she fastened them back on Tavera, the far away look quickly disappearing. "You're bleeding but you're still young." She opened the door to her apartment and went through it.

"I never said I was old," Tavera mumbled after her, following her up the stairs. Old Gam had kind of explained it, in a way. Desire. The way Derk and Gam looked at one another when they thought she wasn't looking. There wasn't anyone she wanted to look at like that but supposedly, it was on its way. They made their way up to the landing and Gam opened the door with her key, making an amused sound once the door swung open. Tavera looked over her shoulder, surprised to see Derk sitting at the table, drinking by himself as he played with a handful of dice by the candle light. Old Gam walked past him towards the bedroom, chuckling.

"I thought you was with Jezlen," Tavera said, sitting down at the table with him. Derk made a face and threw a die at the table, spinning it so that it skipped across the rough surface.

"They got into a fight, like always," Old Gam

said. Tavera could see her pulling off her outdoor clothes and slipping down to her shift. She stood in the doorway, arms over her chest as she looked at them both, eyes narrowed but glinting with merriment.

"We don't always fight, Gam," he said, not looking back at her. He spun all the dice on the table, picking them up and throwing them again, pursing his lips as he did. "I just thought we'd be out later but after a bit he just up and said he had to go somewhere. I already ordered another pitcher even, but still, I couldn't keep him from leaving."

"Where'd he go?" Tavera asked. She'd seen Jezlen several times but never seen his face, which added to his oddity. Gam just sighed and went deeper into the bedroom, fumbling around with her jars of things.

"Who cares, good riddance."

"Oh, Gam, really now!" Derk said, spinning the dice without looking at them. "I still don't know why, after all these years, you STILL don't like him!"

"He doesn't like me!" she retaliated, laughing as she appeared in the doorway again. "I try to be good about it, you've seen."

"You both are horrible at getting on with one another and it's a shame. To think I can't have my two best friends in the same room together without them fighting."

"Aren't you and Gam the ones fighting now?" Tavera said, confused. Derk made a motion to pick up all the dice again but his hand hovered in mid air and he looked to her. A smile cracked his face and he did pick up the dice, tucking them into his belt pouch as he leaned back in his chair.

"Oh, before I forget, Jezlen sent this…for you." He pulled out something from his pack, something long and wrapped in fabric. The fabric itself was nice, a dark green with brown threads sewn into it so that it changed color if you moved it a certain way. Tavera took it and unwrapped the present slowly, her eyes growing big as she realized it was a shortsword. Even Derk whistled upon seeing it, sitting up in his chair to get a closer look.

Tavera looked it over. It wasn't the nicest sword she had seen but it was definitely the nicest one she had ever touched. It was obviously not from the Valley; the slight bend in the scabbard told her that much and the designs on the hilt were not like those of the guards who kept watch on the roads and at the gates. She wrapped her hand around the hilt and pulled gently, sliding it out against her lap. It shone as if it were new and it felt good in her hand, the metal and inlay warming to her touch.

"Tits, Jezlen just got me a new pipe for my last name day and I've saved his life countless times!" Derk said, laughing. Old Gam reappeared from the back room and scoffed, walking into the kitchen to see what Tavera had gotten.

"It's nice but it's hardly fitting for the occasion,"

Old Gam said. Tavera let the shortsword fall back into the scabbard, the metal sliding swiftly in with a satisfying sound. Derk rubbed his face with his hand and stood up from the table, gathering his things and making his way to Gam's room.

"He said it was perfect for this occasion," he called, throwing his things about the bedroom. "He said she can use it for beating back the men that will want her, now that she's of age."

Gam just made a sound and walked after Derk into the room, the blond thief promptly popping out of the room to check on Tavera again. "You'll be alright out here in the kitchen, right?" He looked hopeful and in good spirits, despite his disappointment at his friend having abandoned him for an unsaid purpose.

"Yeah, just go away already, I've been tired since I woke this morning!" she urged, gesturing for him to leave. He didn't go into the room. Derk stepped into the kitchen and walked up to Tavera, looking her over again. He kissed her on the forehead and this time, Tavera rolled her eyes, laughing before she kissed him back on the neck, hugging him where she sat. He said his good nights and ducked into the room, pulling the curtain that separated the rooms across the doorway. Tavera sighed. The bedroll still had to be put out but at least it would be warmer in Gam's house than out in the woods. The shortsword clinked as she picked it up, the weight of it feeling good in her hands. Still holding the blade in one hand, she got her bed ready, not bothering to be quiet. She knew Old Gam and Derk would be listening in the next room, waiting for her to fall asleep. Tavi yawned loudly as she settled into bed, laying the weapon by her head. Before she could even think to strain her ears to hear what Derk and Gam were whispering in the other room, she had fallen asleep.

The next day was the same as any other day waking up at Old Gam's except that Derk had a black eye. Tavera lay in bed until Old Gam came out and chided her for being lazy, the girl scrunching up her face at the woman as her hostess started breakfast. Then Derk came out of the backroom, the hollow of his left eye discolored. It looked like it hurt. Tavera narrowed her eyes at him but he shook his head ever so slightly and then smiled. "Good morning, everyone!" he said, smacking Gam on the backside playfully. Gam swatted him away and he stumbled over to a seat at the table, resting his chin in his hand. He looked tired. Tavera got out of bed and pushed her blankets and roll into a pile, setting her pack and new sword on top before she sat down beside him.

Breakfast was toast and hot milk sweetened with honey and berries to dunk it in. Tavera found her appetite returned and she ate her bread and half of Derk's portion. When her eyes searched around for more food, Old Gam offered her some sausage saying it would be good for her Red Earth time and Tavera felt all the food in her stomach threaten to boil out of her. Derk refused the sausage for her and asked for some tea.

This time Old Gam had a cloth bundle of pastries for Derk on their departure but she had a belt for Tavera, a woman's belt. It was grey with green leaves embroidered into it and meant to tie under her bust, or where a bust should be. There was something there but Tavera didn't think a belt would help. It was however very pretty, as all things that Old Gam crafted were. "Don't wear it now," Old Gam said, playing with Tavera's hair. "Be sure to take it easy today and eat some meat if you can." Old Gam kissed Derk before they left and he winced, her fingers brushing his bruised face.

"Did you go out after I fell asleep?" Tavera asked as they walked down the road. Her sword was in her pack, the hilt sticking out of the top but wrapped with a skirt to hide its true form. Derk took a bite out of a piece of charred meat before he handed the stick over to Tavera, licking his fingers clean of the grease.

"No," he said simply after he was done chewing.

"Well, did you fall into something? It's dark back there," she offered, mouth full of food. Tavera pressed her lips together as Derk gave her a look. She swallowed as quickly as she could without choking. "Did a spirit punch you in the face while you slept? Did you steal something bad? I heard a story once where a man stole from an old shrine and in the night, a spirit pulled down his pants and-"

The look Derk gave her made her stop talking. Tavera gulped as they walked down the street, turning her attention to the goings on of the town this early morning. Her stomach didn't hurt as much as it had yesterday so the smells weren't as offensive to her nose. She took another bite of the food and chewed it thoughtfully, trying not to anger Derk again with messy habits. Tavera heard Derk sigh beside her.

"It was just Gam, Kiff," he said, loud enough for her to hear. "We got into a fight after you passed out. It happens." They both walked quietly down the noisy streets. Tavera finished her food and threw the stick to the ground, trying to think of what to say next.

"Well, did you hit her back?" she asked. It seemed like a good question.

"What? No! Why would I hit Old Gam back?"

"She hit you, didn't she?"

"Kiff, I would never hit Old Gam," he insisted.

"That's probably why she hit you, then." Tavera jumped up on a curb and stepped with one foot in front of the other, feeling the weight of her pack starting to make the straps dig into her shoulders. She hoped they would be taking a cart somewhere. They were supposed to be heading north according to what Derk told Old Gam but that could be a town or the next barony. Tavera looked to Derk again and he was wincing, although Tavi felt it was not from the pain but from a thought in his head. He reached over and yanked her off the curb, hugging her close to him and pulling her hair over her ear. "What did you fight over?" she asked.

"What we always fight over. Friends, money. Connections." Tavera felt like he was going to say 'you' but he held the word back and just squeezed her shoulder. Tavera frowned. Who did Old Gam think she was, hitting her pa like that? She regretted not bringing it up at breakfast despite Derk's silent insistence that she keep quiet. With Tavera watching maybe she could have found something out, get to the heart of the matter between Old Gam and Derk. Years of history was the basis of the relationship of the two adults but maybe a fresh set of eyes could see something they were blind to. Then again Old Gam did just see her as a child, despite the physical change. They came to the gate, the departing carts lined up according to their destinations. Derk led her not towards the northern bound carts but the ones headed east, across the Freewild. Tavi looked up to him and grinned, Derk returning her grin with a wink.

"Just you and the girl?" the woman asked. Her brown hair was very short and her arms were thick with muscles. She even had a tattoo on her forearm that made Tavera's eyes big, a naked woman dancing under the moon. The man behind her was loading bags onto the cart, lashing them down with ropes.

Among the provisions were a few weapons, probably meant more for dealing with issues in the Freewild than for trade. Tavera felt her heart thump with excitement, wanting to leap up onto the cart.

"Aye, to the first eastern village," Derk said, setting his pack on the ground. He pulled out the bundle of pastries Old Gam had made them and a few handfuls of coins. He looked at the provisions on the cart and smiled. "This is headed to Reedwood, ain't it?"

"Right you are," the woman said and she smiled broadly at them. "Lucky for them Portsmouth temple owes them for the manuscripts that burned a few phases ago. Reedwoods crops have been faring poorly these past seasons."

"I've done temple work before, before the library of Reedwood got the annex. We got the Everlight Chalice back from those sunny hem-chewers years ago," Derk said which made Tavera raise her brows. Derk had worked for the church before? This was news to her. Apparently it was good news to the cart driver since she grinned widely.

"Oh, another fellow used to knocking heads in the Green, eh? Well, you're welcome on board, a fellow hand to the temple, past or present." She set her brown eyes on Tavera and looked to her. "And you, can you hold your own if we get into trouble in the Green? You look too young to have helped anyone but yourself."

"I gave him that black eye!" Tavera exclaimed,

which made the large woman laugh so raucously Tavera thought she would never stop. Tears streamed down her face and the woman smacked her on the shoulder, which hurt. She hit hard and Tavera was glad the woman seemed so jovial.

"I like you, little one," the woman proclaimed, crossing her arms over her muscled breasts. She smiled when she said it and Tavera smiled back, deciding she liked her too. The woman gave them a discount on their fare but said they had to acquire their own food and keep watch. Any disobedience meant being left in the Freewild. Derk gave her coin but not the pastries, much to Tavera's delight before they climbed into the cart, settling in among the beans, barley and dried fish.

"You never told me you worked for the church," Tavera said, eating a pastry. Derk just shrugged and pulled out his cards, shuffling them against his knee. Tavera crammed the rest of the food into her mouth and ignored Derk's disapproval, waiting for him to deal her a hand. Excitement, not pain rumbled her stomach now. The Freewild and then the Eastern Valley. She had never been there before. Derk told Old Gam they were heading north. Tavera picked up her cards and didn't care that she had a bad hand. The discomfort of her Red Earth time was stamped out by the prospect of new towns to explore and Derk getting away from Old Gam. Tavera smiled at her pa and laid down a card. The ring around Derk's eye was starting to get more purple and he winced when he smiled back but he seemed in good spirits. There would be plenty of time to win at cards on the journey, Tavera told herself and she set down another card, too happy to care that she would probably lose.

Chapter 7
Something For Nothing

Tavera wasn't wearing her belt on purpose. She could have worn it but Derk had said Shot would be there with Lights and she would have to make an impression so the accessory was left in the room. It was brown, soft leather, rather plain though she had found some pretty green beads to tie at the ends of the laces that kept it tied under her chest. Tavera wore the loosest tunic she had and a skirt and as she leaned over the game board, she could see Lights' dark eyes straying, trying to look down her shirt. The tunic was a bit too big in the shoulders, meant to show the collar bones as was the style. It draped past her shoulder, her brown skin a splash of color in the otherwise drab room. Her dark, thick hair brushed her shoulders and she put it behind her good ear, smiling at Lights.

Tavera took him in when she had first seen him so she could spend the rest of the meeting distracting him and listening to the adults. Shot was there, Derk was there, a red-headed woman who went by Drink was there, all of them looking over a map of the city drawn in chalk on the wooden table in the center of the room. Drink had drawn it and was doing most of the talking, the person in the group who had spent the most time in the spice towns of Redtree, Truehome and Spicehill. The take was for just that: spices. It was high summer and hot in the room. Tavera took another sip of the ale Shot brought. It tasted like healer's hand, spicy but sweet and she took a gulp of it, wiping her mouth with her hand.

It wasn't that Lights wasn't good looking. Dirty blond curls framed his face and he had dark brown eyes. Almost a pretty boy except he tended to have a melancholy air about him that some found off-putting. Derk had told Tavera where Shot had found him and that he wasn't supposed to tell her but it hadn't been so far-fetched. Shot had been at the 'men's home' for a business meeting and found the boy there, serving drinks. Lights looked like the kind of boy a man could desire though the looks he was giving her told her he didn't think of men the same way. Tavera thought he was cute but he didn't make her face hot. And she wasn't there to look at boys, she was there to work.

Spicehill actually had a wall around it with gates

that opened and closed. There were roads common folk weren't allowed to walk on unless they had a pass and ones they were forbidden from completely. The places where the redtree groves and blacknut vines grew were also guarded and anyone who worked there was checked before they left to be sure they weren't stealing anything. The lake grew large aquatic flowers in various colors, the silvery-grey ones prized for making incense for the temples, the roots to make a potent, mind-altering tea reserved only for priest-esses. Redtree also had a wall around it but not the variety of spices for trade and Truehome held the Baron Mielkin's urban home, the grounds dotted by dozens of beehives supplying some of the most inter-esting honeys in the Valley.

Drink was going over the gates of Spicehill, the schedules for the openings and closings of each one, the number of guards and the proximity of the gates to the spice stores and warehouses. The three block lords were not to be trusted. The trio kept itself in bal-ance to the benefit of them all and wouldn't tip their scales for fear of winding up with less in hand than the others. If they caught wind of any plan, they would be after them and on them. In addition, the guards also possessed special dogs at the gates that could sniff out spices.

Tavera listened to all their ideas, talking over the various shop owners and processors of the spice. She moved her game piece on the board, seeing Lights smirk as he captured one of her pieces. A look of disappointment crossed her face and she shrugged. "Can't you go easy on me?"

"Have you ever played Foxes before?" Lights asked, looking down her shirt again. Tavera didn't understand what he was staring at. There was nothing there to see, nothing to warrant that much staring. She knew, she looked at them every day. Maybe Tavera was wrong about Lights; maybe he was into men. She should have worn britches in that case.

"A few times. I like cards more." The group was now talking over the strength of the wall, weak points in the masonry, places where it would be easier to climb.

"Did you bring any cards?" Lights had a fine voice that was almost done with changing, most of his speaking tones deeper rather than higher, a pleasant sound. He could probably get a job as a singer in a hall as long as the change didn't treat him too unkindly. It hadn't thus far. Tavera shook her head and lay on her belly, propping her chin against her hands as she looked over the board. The tones of the adults were starting to sound more exasperated, Derk circling the table with one arm crossed over his chest, one hand at his chin. Drink was refilling in a few spots that Hock had rubbed out with his finger.

"You know, I'm from the southern Valley," Lights said, obviously trying to make conversation. He watched her hand as she moved her dam to protect the kits, leaving her sire wide open. He went in for the kill, killing her sire with his own, removing the piece of carved wood from the board.

"You don't say?" she asked, shifting on her elbows. It was hard to lay like this, the hard floor against her stomach and hipbones and she sat up finally, taking another gulp of her drink. Tavera had pretty much lost the board game but she didn't mind. They hadn't been playing for money and if she had played her cards right, she'd come out on top in the long run.

"Yeah," he answered back. And that was all he replied. Tavera stared at him, expecting him to say something more but realizing he knew he had nothing to say. He wasn't from Spicehill so he couldn't show her around. And he may have been born in the south but it meant nothing now except that he might have a higher tolerance for finger peppers. He smiled at her finally, a nice smile and for a breath Tavera felt a bit guilty. Here they were, two children, two apprentices in the same line of work and instead of trying to make a friend of him, she had tried to distract him, throw him under for her own gain. But then he looked to her chest again and she didn't feel as bad anymore.

"Kiff," Derk called, and he gestured for her to come over. She smiled at Lights before she stood up, shaking out her skirts as she took the few steps to bring her to Derk's side. She looked to where his attention was. "Kiff, what do you see here?"

Tavera had heard all that they had said about the wall, the ways that were barred to them, the locks, the dogs, the punishments. "I see…that maybe we have to have someone else do our taking for us."

Hock placed his hands on the table. Sweat was starting to gather under his armpits and his sweaty knuckles smudged the chalk where his skin touched it. "How do you mean, girl?"

"Well, there's so much watching on the walls and around the town," she said. Her fingers played with the collar of her tunic as she tried to organize the thoughts she had formed during her board game, when Lights had been too busy staring at her and winning. "The best way would be to wait till someone from without came to get their own, left and take it from them. The guards keep logs of everyone coming into town, and how long they'll here. How hard would it be to get a log, look it over for a mark, return it and then head out?" Tavera remembered how they had to state their business and an estimated length of time they planned to be in the city, a gate tax asked from the both of them. The guard assured them that there would be a hefty fee added if they stayed longer than they said, handing them a scrap of fabric with a picture on it. If they lost the fabric they would get another fine. Derk had grumbled about it the entire time they walked to the inn, still muttering about it as he sat over a mug of needleleaf beer. Of all the people who had come for the take, Shot and Lights had put in for the shortest amount of time, all of them giving a different length so as not to draw suspicion.

All of the adults looked at one another. Tavera could almost hear a buzzing as their eyes all flashed round, trading thoughts with looks, all of their eyes looking at her occasionally. Drink smirked at Tavera. "It's hardly glamorous. Road robbery."

"You didn't ask me for the most glamorous. You asked what I'd do. I'd go this way, which still gets me a good bit. People who come through here to buy don't leave with enough for a bowl of bone and broth, they leave with a good amount, they spend a grip or two to take back." Tavera was fairly certain that she had heard that those who traded in Spicehill usually served whole towns or came with the money of several people at a time. Spicehill could guard what was within the walls but they couldn't afford escorts for everyone who came to buy and not everyone who came to buy would come with bodyguards and swords. "If you want glorious, go to Truehome and set fire to the Baron's keep with him inside, start a riot so that the pickers and the guards can have free reign of the fields and the warehouses." Tavera shrugged. "Are we looking for glory or spices?"

Hock laughed out loud, his shoulders shaking. Tavera looked to Derk. His mouth was covered with his hand but he was looking at her with some kind of emotion. She couldn't tell if it was pride or disapproval. Drink looked to Lights, who was still sitting in front of the game, his face blank. Tavera was confused. Had she given the wrong answer? Finally Derk smiled at her and patted her on the shoulder before all the adults broke away from the map and started talking among themselves.

"I'm headed to the Two Headed to have a drink with Hock. Will you clean the map and meet me up there when you're done?" Derk asked. Everyone else was gathering up their things, making plans. Lights got up and threw the game board into his pack, giving Tavera a look she couldn't decipher just yet and she nodded at Derk. "You did alright, Kiff," he smiled again, turning to leave with everyone else. He looked back at her one more time before he disappeared out the door, his big boots stomping heavily down the steps.

Tavera stood there for a moment, wondering what just happened. She shook her head free of the questions and looked down to the ground, finding a bucket of water and a cloth. Sweat dripped down her side as she dipped the cloth in, wringing it out over the wooden table. The water splattered and made dark circles on the wooden surface, making spots on her tunic and brushing against her skin when she moved. Tavera sighed as she wiped away at the chalk marks on the table, destroying the evidence scrawled there. The white chalk buried deep into the wood and so she had to drown it out with big scoops of water, spreading it out so it would dry quickly in the heat. A lock of hair fell into her eyes and she pushed it away, wetting it with her hands in the hopes it would stay back. She looked at the table and then back at the bucket. She would need more water.

The stable boy at the inn traded her empty bucket for a full one and she flashed him a smile that made him grin back, heading back up towards the staircase leading up to the little room. A familiar head of curls caught her eye and followed her but she didn't bother to turn and acknowledge him, keeping her eyes forward.

"Hey," Lights said when she was halfway up the stairs, his gaze set on her. She tossed her head at him and continued up to the room, careful not to spill the water. Tavera didn't bother closing the door. She knew he would close it when he got to the room and he did, a quiet thud punctuating his arrival.

"I know you tricked me into not paying attention at the meeting," he shot at her. Tavera rolled her eyes and dipped the cloth into the bucket, squeezing it onto the table again.

"I'm not the one who was so taken by hardly nothing at all," she said, mocking him with her tone. "Besides, no one asked for your input, so no one found out you've got nothing in your head but eyes and a tongue. Though I'm sure your pa noticed Hock didn't so much as look at you the whole time." She looked over her shoulder, expecting him to look angry or even embarrassed. Instead the young man looked distressed, his eyes lost as his thoughts rattled in his brain.

"He's not my pa," he answered finally and she thought she heard him choke, a crack in his voice giving away his age. "And asides, you and the Lurk ain't fooling anyone. Who do you think you are? You're just another set of hands to tear out a share, you know! And not for who you think, neither! Hock's just using everybody to get what he wants, and you included!"

"That ain't true," Tavera snapped and she wheeled around, forgetting her duties and focusing her anger on Lights. "You think you know better than me? I've known Hock longer than you, I've known Derk longer than you!" Tavera's brain scrambled as she tried to think of something to shoot at him, to knock him down before he carried this too far. "Though I suspect you do know men better than me! Shot's said as much to everyone."

Light's eyes went wide, as if he'd been kicked between the legs and his face went white and then red. His mouth disappeared on his face as he pressed his lips together. Lights swallowed and then he blew his breath out quietly, as if exhaling the words he wanted to say. "That...that is how I know this, Kiff. I've known men like Hock. He's like a priestess with a knife for a twixt, you pull up her robes and you're dead! He'll use your pa too and he's already using you."

"Why're you talking about The Cup like this!? You know The Cup ain't bad! Not bad for people like us. We need it. My pa ain't bad for people like us."

"Your pa is fine, The Cup is fine, I've nothing against stealing and having fun! Just because we live by the take doesn't mean we shouldn't take pride as well as blueies! But Hock...I...Kiff..." He sat on the floor cross legged, and put his head into his hands, his blond curls spilling over his fingers. For a moment Tavera thought that he was laughing but after a few breaths she took a step back, realizing that he was crying. "I just...I don't want to be used anymore, Kiff? Do you?"

Tavera frowned and set the cloth down on the table before she walked over to him as quietly as she could, sitting besides him. His face was covered with his hands but she put her hand on his chin and made him look at her.

"No," she said, her dark eyes looking into his. Tavera felt like crying too but couldn't. She sat next to Lights and let her hands fall into her lap, feeling his eyes still on her, the hot day made even warmer by how close they sat to one another. Tavera stared down at her hands, long, brown fingers made soft by rubbing them with oil every night. Was that all she was? A pair of hands? No. Did Hock think that? Let him think that. If at first he accepted her hands, he might accept the rest of her, wouldn't he? Everything in small steps. Hock was learning she could take and also deal, everyone at the table had seen it. Derk knew it. He knew that and more.

"Lights, Hock…just…be yourself and do a good job. Hock'll come around. Shot's not a bad guy, though he's a bit…gruff." Tavera smiled at Lights and he smiled back at her, his long-lashed eyes looking pretty despite the tears. She found herself biting the inside of her lip as he leaned in closer, his warm breath brushing against her mouth before he kissed her. Tavera closed her eyes and let him, returning the kiss once she thought he wouldn't push her away and he didn't. Instead he put an arm behind her and leaned into her more, kissing her, his tongue slipping into her mouth. It made her pull away at first but when he kissed her again she didn't stop him this time and she opened her mouth, trying the same and deciding that she liked it.

His hand went under her tunic and slid up her belly to her chest, his hand proving that there was something there after all. Tavera's body tingled as he touched her, and she tried to figure out what to do with her hands. This was usually the part where Derk would walk by and grab her by the arm, yanking her away from the boy she had been kissing. She wasn't a stranger to boys but having a boy all to herself, and a boy that knew her, knew her really…it made things different. It made Tavera put her hands under his tunic and pull it over his head and she bit his lip without knowing why she did it.

His hand went up her skirt, his fingers kneading at her skin and then pulling off her shirt and she trembled despite the heat, letting him lay her back on the floor. It was still wet in spots from when she had been washing the table clean and for a second she wondered if she had cleaned it enough. But the thought was quickly chased away by Lights bending over her, his melancholy face now warm and happy as he kissed her again, his belt coming away from his britches in her hands and more of his skin pressing against hers, the hard floor under her.

In the end Tavera found herself washing blood from her legs and looking over at Lights, his back to her as he buttoned his pants and put on his tunic again. Tavera thought as she washed up, wiping her face with clean water, feeling a touch of an ache in her lower belly, wondering if that was what it was supposed to be like. What part of it had been desire, and what had she really desired? Lights? He was handsome, she supposed. His hands and his other parts on her skin and inside of her?

It made her head swim a bit to think about it, and her stomach fluttered, tugging on the corners of her mouth so that she was smiling at her reflection in the bucket. It wasn't the most fun thing she had done but many things weren't the first time and Derk seemed to enjoy himself anytime they crossed paths with Old Gam. In the end, after Lights had kissed her more awkwardly than she had ever been kissed before and left her, she thought she wouldn't have paid money for it but she'd be willing to give it another go.

"What happened to you?" Derk asked when she slid into her seat at the bar. "You fall into the bucket?" He was sitting alone at the Two Headed, the ale almost gone in the pitcher. He poured her a mug. It sloshed over the side and onto the table, fizzing there. Tavera just shook her head and took the mug, looking into it before she took a big gulp. It was sweet and spicy.

"You did good today, girl," Derk said, smiling drunkenly. He patted her on the head and drained his mug, pouring himself the rest of the pitcher as he looked to her. "Real good."

"So they're using my plan?" She wondered if she and Derk would get in on the take. If they used her plan, would she get any of the rewards? Tavera knew a few places that spices could be unloaded quietly, a few kitchens and a few individuals who would trade for a finger's worth of redtree bark or a blacknut or three.

Derk shook his head. "Not exactly, but something like it. We're hanging about for a few days to read the guards, get information but Drink's got something invested in this and Hock…." Derk shrugged. "But he said your idea was a good one." He drank the rest of his pitcher and looked to her, woozily. Blond lashes blinked slowly and he made a face at her. "Are you feeling well, Kiff? You look all…" All he could do was gesture towards her with his hands and make pained, drunken faces. Tavera felt her face get hot and she lowered her head, hunching her shoulders to make herself smaller, so there'd be less of her to read.

"I'm fine, Derk. You're just drunk." Tavera frowned at him, wondering if he could tell. He had slept with women. Maybe he could tell, just like he could tell what kind of thief someone was just by the way he walked. She didn't feel different. Just sore.

"I'm not...you're right, I am drunk." Derk laughed and shook his head, lacing his fingers together and putting them behind his head. He smiled dimly, which made her roll her eyes. "I was thinking we could head to the west side after this."

"Not north?" Tavera asked, raising her eyebrows. Ravinewild was north, and Moorland. Derk's face became muddled and he looked as if he might be sick, burping quietly.

"No. In two days. I mean, we'll head north first and then west. With Shot and Lights. At first light. Heh." Derk put his hand on the table and pushed himself up, chuckling over his rather bad joke. "They're staying at the inn across from the north well." He managed to lean forward without toppling over and kissed her on the top of her head, leaving a few coins to pay for the drinks and a bit extra for her. Then he left, stumbling out of the bar without knocking into anyone. Tavera watched him go.

She ordered a bowl of stew and ate it, thinking over the events of the day. So, Hock had liked her plan? And Derk knew he did. But what about Drink and Shot? Drink had criticized her, saying her plan wasn't glamorous enough. Well, Tavera wasn't there to please Drink. She was there to come up with a plan that they could pull off and keep them out of the clacks. The beer they served in the Spicehill dregs was the same as the beer anywhere else, she reasoned, drinking from her mug. Her thoughts strayed to Lights, wondering what he thought of her plan. They were in the same spot after all. One day they could be sitting across the table from one another, making plans, criticizing one another, relying on the other's skills. She scraped up the last bit of her stew with her spoon and stood up, deciding that maybe she should find out what Lights thought of her plan.

The inn by the north well was called the North Well Inn, and she found their room after asking the boy turning the spits where the boy with the blond hair was staying. The spit turner told her and then asked if she would rather know where he was staying and she laughed, swishing her skirts flirtatiously as she made her way towards the room. Maybe, she told herself. They'd be there a few more days.

A quick knock on the door brought the sound of footsteps and the door cracked open, dark brown eyes looking at her. He opened the door and she slipped in, Lights closing the door behind her.

"Everything alright?" he asked. Tavera had gone there meaning to ask him about her plan and what he had thought about it. But then she remembered how he felt about Hock and what his skin felt like and tried hard not to grin, her hands behind her back.

"Where's Shot?" she asked, looking around the room. Shot and Lights were messier than she and Derk, clothes hanging off of things, their packs undone and laying slopping on the floor. Lights scratched his head and shrugged, looking confused.

"He's out with Drink, why?" he asked.

"I want to try again," she said, her words more forceful than she had intended them to be. For a breath Lights looked confused and they stared at each other for a moment, his eyes growing bigger as he realized what she was asking. He fumbled to secure the door, looking around the room as if someone else was there watching before his mouth met hers, Tavera pulling him with her towards the unmade bed.

It always took a few times to get something right, Tavera told herself. The first time she stole a tart she burned her fingers and it had broke in her hands as she ran away. The first time she had thrown a punch, she scraped her knuckles so badly they had bled. Tavera won a small victory, gaining a bit of Hock's acceptance, even if Drink didn't approve of her plan so a bit of celebration was in order, right? A memory from her days with Prisca came to mind and she pushed Lights onto the bed before he could push her, sitting on top of him. This time would be better, she thought.

Tavera pushed through the crowd, smiling at the bearded man who brushed up against her, his hand squeezing her backside in the press of people. Her hand squeezed too but her fingers wrapped around the coins he had in his pocket, the only thing about him she found interesting and he laughed, thinking something else. It was hot in the bar, people singing and drinking and carrying on. It was High Summer Moon and out of doors people were splashing each other with buckets of water in celebration, drinking barley water and beer indoors, playing music on every street corner.

Derk let her run about town to partake in the festivities and Tavera had loosed herself on the town of Redbriar as if it were her last day on earth. The heat and the holiday gave everyone free reign and people ate, drank and caroused to their hearts desire, the gluttony of heat calling for a gluttony of the body. She had already been drenched by two buckets of water and personally seen to the dousing of three guards, laughing hysterically as the water dripped through their light armor and pooled beneath them.

She was returning from the temple where the priestesses had moved a statue of the goddess outside, the grey clad women standing around and accepting donations of money, food and other things, the surplus of the season going to the temple in thanks to the White Breasted One. Even the statue of the goddess and the priestesses were not exempt from the buckets of water, water dripping down the white, clay folds of her garments. Some of the priestesses were drenched while the dry ones looked at the wet ones enviously. The day was sweltering and all the open windows and door didn't help to dispel the heat of the grips of people pressed against each other, dancing, singing, drinking, groping.

All the inns were full to capacity for the holiday and she and Derk had been staying in a common room with a dozen other people, the sleeping habits of strangers and the excitement for the holiday having made it difficult to go to sleep the previous night. But this morning's sleepiness was chased away by good cheer and she slapped a blueie on the counter, the bartender offering her a pitcher of the the weak beer everyone drank in great volumes today. She shook her head and mouthed what she wanted and the bartender put a hand to his ear, leaning forward to try and hear her. She shouted her order and he nodded, reaching behind the bar for a glass and the green bottle that held the liquor she was seeking. The liquor itself was green and it sparkled as he poured it. Tavera reached over with both hands and wrapped her fingers around it, pushing her way past the people to the staircase in the back that went down to the basement.

The noise in the basement didn't match the din upstairs but it was just as hot and smokier. Card tables were set up and people were betting money, pieces of fabric, thread, dried goods, anything they had that was acceptable to the other players. She looked around, the smoke from the pipes swirling before the light the lanterns gave off. Men and women were playing and kissing and cursing and singing. Derk had been here when he had cut her loose and she thought she would find him here again, but her eyes found nothing but strangers. A face she recognized brought her over to the table and she couldn't help but gaze at the man's cards.

"Where's my pa?" she asked. The man arranged his cards and threw in two blessed candles from the Holy Bowl, a good bet indeed.

"Who, the yellow haired hem chewer who took me for ten fullies and five lengths of ribbon? Are the ribbons for you, girl?" The balding man looked up at her, his beard crawling across his face like a rash. "I suppose not. Hair like a boy. Tits like one too."

"D'you know where he is or don't you?" she shot, annoyed. He laughed and threw down two cards and picking up another two.

"He left a bit ago, someone gave him a whisper and he got a stony face and shot off. Now, be gone with you, girl!"

Tavera glowered at him, glad Derk had beat him at cards. Still. "He's got three wings," she said to the rest of the table, turning and rushing out before the man could get a hold of her, the sound of chairs overturning and cursing clamoring behind her as she laughed, bolting up the stairs. She pushed her way through the crowd, glad she was tall. Her last growth spurt had put her of a height with Derk though he outweighed her by quite a bit. A hand grabbed her chest and she held her drink over her head as she made her way out, glad to get a lungful of cooler, fresh air. The noise of the outdoor revelries carried up to the sky and Tavera took a sip of her drink. It was herbal and slightly bitter, but good.

Her feet carried her to the temple. It was the only place Derk would find to think if he was in a serious mood. Regardless of the type of worship the day required, temples were always quiet, a place for prayer and contemplation. Tavera barely missed being drenched by a bucket of water as she turned a corner, almost spilling her drink but she dodged the spray of water intended for someone else. The white steps shone in the distance and she poured the rest of her drink at the feet of the statue of the goddess, smiling at the stained figure before she took the steps in twos, looking around for Derk.

He was sitting by himself to the far left, his blond hair unmistakable to the girl. Other people were praying at the altar, a couple ready to take their vows of loyalty there with the ribbon for the priestess to bless. Tavera reached the aisle and slid down the length of the wooden pew on her knees, drawing a disapproving scowl from her father.

His blue eyes were bloodshot. Derk had been crying though he wasn't now. His prayer beads lay laced through his fingers and he bowed his head. For a second Tavera thought he was going back to praying but he squeezed in close next to her and he sighed. "Hock is dead."

"What?" Tavera's mouth dropped open slightly and she looked forward, letting the news sink in. "I'm…I'm sorry, pa."

"You didn't kill him," Derk said, shrugging. His face looked tired, the lines at the corners of his eyes looking deeper, darker. "Nobody killed him. He had a chest pain and…then he couldn't breath. And he died. No knife. No rope. Not even from catching a bad chill." Derk shook his head and looked sad, the saddest she had ever seem him look and it made Tavera uncomfortable. He sucked snot up through his nose and wiped his face with his sleeve, the beads glinting in the light. His blue eyes looked not only sad but confused, Tavera saw.

Hock had been his mentor but also his leader, the unofficial leader of The Cup. Questions shone in his eyes as well as grief and he stared down at his hands, looking to Tavera's. Derk forced a smile, a rather pathetic one. "At least his last take was a good one. The spice bit. That was good, Tavi." His hands reached for hers and she let him take them, wrapping his fingers through them. "Tavera, you must promise me something."

"What, pa?" The beads from the rosary dug into her skin and his grip was tight. He held her hands tighter still and he lowered his voice so that she had to lean in to hear it.

"Promise me now, in front of the goddess that if something should happen to me...if I should be caught by guards or a lord or anyone...you will not come for me."

"What?"

"Promise me," he whispered. "I didn't pluck you from that woman, I didn't raise you in my eyesight, share my bed, my food, my secrets, my friends...for you to wind up in jail besides me. I would die if that happened, Tavi. My heart would tear in two."

"Derk, you won't get caught, you can't-"

"Tavi, it could happen. Everyone makes mistakes. And sometimes things just...they just happen." He sighed wearily and he kissed her on the cheek, a dry, fatherly kiss that made tears well up in her eyes. "Please, Tavi. Promise."

Tavera swallowed hard, trying to get rid of the quiver that threatened her voice and she nodded, focusing on the pain of the beads digging into her skin. "I promise, Derk. I'll always be your girl. And if it happens...I'll keep on being your girl." It was hard to say and the words tried not to come but they did. The relief in Derk's face made it worth it. He let go of her hands finally, pulling her to lay on his shoulder. He smelled like tobacco smoke and beer and sweetsleep and he played with her hair, careful not to expose her ear. Her tears drained away and she looked up at the goddess that stood before them indoors, her black hands offering abundance to her worshipers. "What now? With the Cup?" she asked.

She felt his shoulder shrug under her head, his free hand playing with the beads of his rosary, more for something to do than out of piety. "Everyone will stumble around for a bit. There'll be some arguments. But eventually everyone will come together again. Someone will rise above the others and take the lead. Same as always."

"Maybe you?" Tavera said, turning her head to look up at him. Derk turned his head to look at her and snorted with laughter. It made a priestess look to them and he mouthed an apology, keeping his chuckles in his chest so that Tavera felt them under her head.

"If you love your pa you'll never wish that on me," he said. "No, someone else. Luckily I was on the upswing when he left. It could have gone badly for us. No, I won't ever be the head but I can be on a shoulder. In good graces. I think we're there now." He smiled at her and mussed her hair which made her make a face. They sat there in the temple for a while, breathing in the incense and listening to the chimes when she felt Derk draw in his breath before he spoke again. "You slept with Lights?"

Tavera's body stiffened slightly and Derk had his answer. He breathed out his disappointment in one long sigh and Tavera sat up, keeping her eyes on the altar. "It's not a big deal,"she said. "You sleep with Old Gam all the time."

"I...what?" He opened his mouth to yell it but he kept his voice down, the sanctity of the church relegating him to a hiss. "I occasionally keep company with Old Gam, when we cross paths. And I've known Old Gam longer than you've been alive."

"We don't know how long I've been alive so that might not be true."

"You are...you are missing the point." Derk said, as quietly as he could though there was anger in his voice. "I don't want you starting to do this, not now. And not within the Cup."

"Me and Lights aren't in the Cup yet," Tavera pointed out. It made Derk give her an angry look but she cut him off again. "Besides, we're both in the same spot. It's nice to have fun with a...a friend. A real one."

Derk laughed, a sardonic laugh that made heat rise in her cheeks. "Okay, Tavi. You tell yourself that. He's your friend. Not another thief looking to get the upper hand on you, looking out for himself or Shot. I'm offering you the easy answer, trying to guide you to a good decision."

"How d'you know I wasn't trying to get something from him?" Tavera narrowed her eyes at him and Derk just stared at her for a breath before he put his head in his hands, rubbing his eyes with the palms of his hands.

"This is not the conversation I want to be having right now." Derk was about to put the rosary around his neck but he hesitated, looking to his daughter. He put it around her neck and kissed her on the cheek again. It was so chaste it made her face hot again and she let the rosary slip over her head, feeling the carved goddess bead slip over her skin and between her breasts. "Remember what we talked about, please," he said, waving her away. "It's a holy day. Go. Have fun. For me."

"Are you sure?" she asked, grinning. Derk smiled, not as big as she would have liked but it was something.

"No. Yes. I mean," he said, rubbing his face again, shooing her away finally. "Go. You shouldn't be sad today. I shouldn't be but I am. So be happy for us both. You know what I'd be doing. Just…remember we're leaving at the end of second watch tomorrow." He said the last bit too loud and several priestesses quieted him with a stern look, Derk bowing his head in response. Tavera turned and bowed her head as she ducked out, realizing she left her cup in the temple. She shrugged inwardly. The priestesses would clean the temple tomorrow and return the cups to the bars. If they only had to deal with empty cups, it would be a blessing.

Music rang through the air and laughter seemed to come from around every corner, splashes of water and light fighting the heat and darkness of the evening. The full moon rose in the sky, seeming to glow down approvingly at her children's revelries. Tavera tried to smile, but the sober conversation she had just had with Derk kept her steps slow and her mouth from smiling. Hock had died. One day Derk would die or wind up in prison and she would be left alone. Derk had her and the Cup to fall back on, Old Gam, Jezlen when he was around. Her grip on the Cup was tenuous at best and everyone else she knew...Tavera shook her head. Derk was young and while he did do things in excess, he didn't indulge to the point that Hock had. Derk was still active and never complained, hardly getting sick though when he did he was an absolute child.

She smiled remembering the last time he was sick, how pathetic he had been, making Tavera make him tea in just the right way or he couldn't drink it. He'd be around for a while. Tonight they were both alive and Tavera was young. Her eyes fastened on a boy with dark hair and dimples and she smiled to herself, following him to where two roads met, a trio of musicians playing music and townspeople dancing in time. The boy walked over to another young man who had a jug of what could only be wine and she sat down next to him and smiled. The dark haired boy smiled back, his arm quickly wrapping around her waist. He wasn't a thief, she said to herself. She was. Tavera would steal a dance and maybe a bit more in the name of the goddess tonight and since the girl and the deity were the only ones who knew about it, so be it.

Chapter 8
Growing Pains

As the tavern door creaked open, her body barely filled half of the frame, the light from the street having no trouble getting past her as she entered. It was early but the tavern was open for first meal, the smell of yeast and coals filling her nostrils as she inhaled deeply. It was obvious that she was tired. The slender girl walked over to the closest bar stool and promptly set herself on it, laying her head down on the bar top and closing her eyes as she waited for someone to notice she was there so she could ask for some food.

The onset of adolescence had seemed to breathe life into the exotic features of the elves, though it was tempered by the human blood that also ran in her veins. Her hair was dark and cut short, its length barely able to cover her face and carelessness allowing a slightly pointed ear to poke its way through the shorn tresses. Her other ear was a distinguishing feature that was best kept hidden. The pink flesh running completely straight was testament to an injury sustained quite some time ago but was now at least physically healed. Instead of the skirts most women wore she wore dark britches, cuffed at the ends to keep them out of the muck, her other clothes seeming to be men's clothes altered slightly to better suit her body. In truth, from afar she was often mistaken for a man but her face was pretty and definitely feminine. Her large, full mouth parted slightly, a low snore emitting from her nose.

The sound of booted feet didn't disturb her, nor was she woken by the stool next to her being dragged so that someone could sit on it. Only when the same booted foot hooked itself on her seat and pulled it out from under her did she notice and even then, she was too late to make a graceful recovery. She cursed out loud, her dark angry eyes tinged with sleep as well as a touch of fear. No one in the bar looked or paid any mind, the few scant patrons too tired or drunk from last nights endeavors to care.

"You coulda broke my neck," she whispered, not wishing to break the sanctity of the quiet bar in the morning, rubbing her elbow with her hand. The man who sat beside her took a breath as if to speak but caught himself, pressing his thin lips together and rubbing his temples with his hands. His sandy blond hair was now streaked with lines of silver and creases had taken their places in the corners of his blue eyes. He took another deep breath, laying his hands primly on the bar top before he spoke, his words even in tone and volume, though his voice shook with what she knew to be anger.

"You should not have stayed out all night by yourself," was what he said, though she knew he desperately wanted to say more. "I…" He lowered his voice, turning his head slightly towards her, his words coming slightly faster. "I know that I had a bit too much to drink, but you shouldn't take advantage of that. We were the guests of honor and it was rude of you to go."

"You were the guest of honor and I didn't want to sit about, hearing you all rehash the same old bullshit stories I've heard too many times to count. I wanted to have some fun."

"Fun, eh? Did you have your fun with the same playmate as you did two nights ago? Or was it your old pally from last week?" So this was it. The girl turned her head sharply towards him, still keeping her voice down though the air around them seemed hot with their anger.

"So now it's out," she said, almost hissing, the sleep snapped away from her eyes by her ire. "You know what I've been up to and you're mad as piss about it. You're just mad cause you thought coming here would keep me from doing it and it didn't work."

"We came here 'cause a third of the town burned to the ground and the pickings were slim," he said, disbelief at the girl's logic ringing in his voice. "Granted, I thought you'd wait to know the local idiots at least a month before your pants came flying off but I see I was mistaken. And what have I told you about wearing britches in public? It ain't lady like and it'll attract attention, it will."

"I like wearing pants when I'm about, Pa," she said, glad the conversation turned away from the previous topic. She saw the smug look on her father's face as he brought it close to hers, his eyes hard and his breath hot and sour.

"Yes, you must have at least a bit of a challenge for them, make them wait at least as long as it takes to get them around your ankles." Tavera couldn't believe he had just said that to her and for a moment her mouth just popped open and shut, like a fish out of water. She wanted to hit him, she wanted to curse at him and cause a scene but all their arguments were like this: quiet and keen and close. The young woman looked away from him. She knew he had already seen the tears in her eyes and she knew he was sorry for what he said, as good a jab as it had been.

"Look at you, judging me," she said quietly. "You've got a set on you, ain't yah? And here I am, knowing when Hale the jeweler's gonna be out of town on business. What've you got? The shits and an hangover from too much dark ale. You've some nerve, pushing the morals you've picked and chosen on me, pissing all over me when you're the one who dragged me through the streets. Y'know, I ain't stupid. I could've taken up a different profession and maybe done well at it."

"Maybe you could've, but you've the heart of a thief, girl. Anything you put your hand to, you'd have wound up taking wrongfully and been on your way. Don't you see that? You're lucky I got you when I did or you'd be in the clacks." He took in a deep breath, resting his head in his hand as he looked over the girl, her back straight and her eyes avoiding his. "Come now," he said softly, lowering his head as he spoke. "You say you know when Hale'll be out, do you?"

"Oh well this is dovey," she hissed, getting up from her chair. "It ain't right to pick up loose change, 'cept when it adds up to a fullie, is it? Chew Her hems, I'm leaving."

Her father sat up straight in his chair, neither anger nor greed in his voice, "What about breakfast? You need to eat."

"Toss off," she called back, not bothering to turn around. Tavera strode out of the bar and onto the street, the road considerably more busy that it had been just a while ago. Her face felt hot and her own angry thoughts muffled the sounds of the city waking up. Just who did he think he was, telling her what to do and then making it okay if it suited his purposes? It was worse than prostitution! A thief she was, or rather a "thiefling," according to the others they mostly dealt with. She'd been running around in Derk's shadow for almost seven years now and still, she was 'Derk's Kiffer.' She got more respect from the no-talented hacks that preyed upon the sick, poor and stupid than the people who practiced thievery as an art form, the people she was supposedly being taught to emulate, the ones she sided with most.

How she felt after a 'take' proved that she was one of them and not a thug. Tavera relished in the careful planning of the procedure, the consideration of time and place. She looked over and cared for her tools more lovingly than a surgeon cared for his saws and scalpels. The feel of coin or a pretty token in her hand was magnified by the pride she felt by having something she contrived go well. Tavera was in her element when something that did not belong to her was in her hands.

But she didn't understand why it was wrong to be herself, why there were laws meant to bar her from expressing herself in the way she best saw fit. If people had destinies as the temple folk always said and if her destiny was to be a thief, like Derk and in truth, her heart said, why was the fear of the Jugs pushed upon her as a deterrent? Derk said the fear of the Jugs would keep her good at what she did, and it did. She hadn't been apprehended once though she had been chased a few times. All that running Derk made her do when they were in the country came in handy. If

people should fulfill their destinies, who decided if
one destiny was good and left to unfold while another
should be snuffed out or punished?

Her boots stopped as they found themselves in
front of the Temple of the Full Moon. Her adopted
mother always went to the temple when she had had a
bad day and needed to collect her thoughts while
Derk tended to turn his eyes towards the altar for
blessings before carrying out larger plans. The temple
was open, though the front doors were closed
presently, the front steps empty of beggars and children at the moment. Tavera pushed a stray lock of
hair out of her face before starting towards the temple.

"Velida?" Tavera looked around to see who was
calling out, her eyes widening as they fell upon a
blond, handsome young man who was looking directly at her. Velida was the name she was giving in
this town, her real name and handle not an option if
she wanted to make good on an escape. She tried to
remember his name quickly and anything she might
have told him, seeming to remember that he was a
new recruit to the town guard and that his name was
Loren. His name was important but his occupation
would probably prove more fruitful in the near future.

"Lori!" she cried, using a more familiar form of
his name, laughing inwardly as he actually blushed.
Now she remembered him. He had been standing
with a few other young men around his age and they

were all snickering as they pointed and talked, too far for her to listen unless she tried. Tavera focused her attention on the young man, smiling primly once he reached her, dodging a cart full of chickens to get across the street. "Nice t'see you. What are you doing on this end of town?"

"Oh, I'm just here with a few of the boys after morning training," he said, pointing over his shoulder. He had hair the color of corn and faint freckles, his face as honest as a child and his eyes as bright. He was new to the guard and the city, having joined to save money for a home of his own in whatever back-woods farming village he was from. Tavera knew he liked her and while he wasn't stupid, he was as naive as they came. The young man was very handsome and as he smiled helplessly at her, she almost felt guilty for standing as close as she was to him. He put his hands in his pockets, looking her up and down, his hazel eyes filled with curiosity as they fell upon her legs. "Why're you wearing britches?"

"Oh, both my dresses got dirty, one after the other and as they're both in the wash, I had to make do with these. Pardon my shabby appearance!" she said, trying to seem ashamed of her clothes. Boys like him were quick to pay compliments when fished for and if she could endear herself to him and stroke her ego at the same time, why not?

"You look fine in britches, Velida, really. It's just a strange thing to see a woman in 'em and a stranger thing to see a woman look good in 'em." He smiled, proud he had managed to come up with such a phrase and was rewarded with another smile from the half-elf girl. He relaxed slightly, ignoring the hoots his fellows were making behind him, looking at the temple that stood just a few yards away. "You goin' in for worship? I didn't know you were a regular."

"Ah, yeah, well, it's something I do when I've had a rough bit, though it's smoothed out considerably since I got here." Now she was going to stroke his ego, smiling as his cheeks reddened again and he stood up straight, his hands crossing over his chest, his hair flowing behind him in the breeze. For a moment Tavera almost felt embarrassed by how handsome he was, how intently his eyes were fixed on her and not her pants...did he actually like her? He couldn't like her, Tavera; he didn't know Tavera at all and if he did, as a guard and as good as he was, he would most likely arrest her. For the first time in a long while she actually felt uncomfortable in front of someone and her browned face reddened, breaking the intense gaze they had locked.

"Look, I've got to be getting inside...morning prayers are about to start," she said, looking everywhere but at him, taking steps backwards and hoping he wouldn't follow.

"Of course," he said, putting his hands up, seeming embarrassed that he had kept her from her devotions. Her heart was beating hard in her chest, her stomach feeling as if it had a hundred fish swimming inside of it. Was he just going to go? Why did it matter? She knew where he kept guard and knew when he was most likely to be there. Why had seeing him on the street like this flustered her so? She felt like she was going to throw up, spinning on her heel and heading as quickly as she could towards the temple.

"Hold on," she heard, her ear pricking up, finding herself facing him once more. He turned his head to the side as something had suddenly caught his eye before saying, "D'yah think perhaps I could see you another time...like, in the evening? If you were thirsty?"

Tavera thought of a few snotty ways to brush him off and a few coy ways to tell him yes, but none of them seemed right. The bell that signaled morning prayers rang in the Temple of the Full Moon, several other people on the street starting to make their way into the white washed building. "Look, I've gotta... I'll...I'll find you later, right? You have third watch? At the Sheep Gate?"

"Right" he said, his eyebrows raised as if impressed that she remembered, nodding and smiling to himself. "Right, well...see you then."

"Right, yeah...." She couldn't think of anything to say so she turned around and ran up the steps, weaving between other would-be worshipers to get into the temple as quickly as possible. The priestess was already at the dais, silver chalice in hand, her face calm and as round as the full moon, her silver dress tightly laced so that her breasts seemed to almost spill out of the garment.

It wasn't fair, she couldn't help but think as she bowed her head staring down at her own chest. If she had breasts like those she could use half as many words and a quarter as many promises to get men to pay her mind. At least you'll know it's not just their eyes that like you, Derk would say. She didn't want them to like her, she wanted them to want her so she could get information quicker than the others so she could get the take before they did. A fine rack would have come in handy but that she lacked so she made up for it with a pretty face, slick words and promises of things to come. But that boy outside...the priestess had raised the chalice now and was speaking the prayer, invoking the goddess to turn her eyes towards her people, her pale hands gripping the silver cup, the scant sunlight glinting off of it...was it really made of pure silver?

Tavera cursed herself, pushing thoughts of taking the sacred cup aside, reminding herself of its role, of what might befall the temple and the worshipers if the consecrated item was missing. She really was a thief through and through, more than she was a worshiper of the goddess of the moon or a girl to take out for beers or someone to spend an evening with, or at least a few moments.

Should she go out with that boy who watched the gates? The priestess lowered the chalice, beckoning the worshipers to come forward, the bodies shuffling out of the pews and queuing in the main aisle. Tavera bit her lip as she approached, keeping her head down and her eyes closed as she moved forward, trying to keep her mind focused on her prayers and the task to come. Should she go out with Lori?

After what seemed like an eternity, she reached the alter and looked towards the priestess. The priestess' face was calm to the point of seeming unnatural, her grey eyes emotionless, her face as steady as a bust of marble. Tavera kept her eyes locked with the priestess, the goddess' avatar on earth, dipping her fingers into the chalice, bringing it to her forehead and then placing her wet fingers into the bowl that lay on the altar. She knew the goddess answered in riddles so she didn't think of any questions as she placed the tips of her fingers in the bowl, the fingers that had stolen many things over the last few years. She instead laid to rest that which she wanted to strike from herself, as she was supposed to do.

Her strange new emotions for Loren, she left in the bowl. Her contempt for the other members of the Cup who didn't yet accept her as one of their own. And her wanton ways that made her father give her looks that distressed her…she lifted her fingers from the bowl, which was full of strange, grey sand, not bothering to wipe the odd powder from her fingers as she returned to her seat. The rest of the congregation filed through, performing the same ritual. When the last worshiper had performed the rite, the priestess spoke the words Tavera was glad to hear, raising the chalice above her head and tipping it, the liquid contents of the chalice streaming down in a silver ribbon, the contents of the bowl inundated with the libation. A bell rang from somewhere within the building and the priestess spoke, her voice low and even.

"Now are our secrets hidden in the bosom of our goddess, swept up in her watery arm and brought close to her heart that we may be free of their burden. Go forth, knowing your secrets are safe, knowing you are free to change if that is what is in your destiny. Go in grace, unburdened by your troubles. Go with love, knowing the goddess delights in the workings of our hearts." The bell rang again and the priestess bowed her head, signaling that the worshipers were now free to leave as they saw fit.

Morning prayers were the best, Tavera thought as she exited the building. She always felt lighter after morning prayers and liked the crowd that typically showed up at the first worship. Vespers were full of the more devoted individuals who came to pay tribute to the goddess of the moon, the White Lady who opened the Valley for them all those generations ago, keeper of secrets, bringer of change, reveler in love. The mornings were full of those who came for penance, most of them coming to service before going to bed for the day, coming in from the street after a night of performing things that warranted covering up. The girl scanned the street for the boy she was considering having a drink with. Maybe it was for the best he was gone. Maybe she wouldn't pass by the Sheep Gate during his watch but instead avoid him for the rest of their stint in this city. It was doable. But was it what she wanted? Did he only have freckles on his nose?

Both hands were brought to her head and she ruffled her hair as she mumbled to herself, trying to push her thoughts on the farm boy away. Sleep would help. If her mind was fresh she could keep her thoughts from wandering. The bed above the inn sounded wonderful. But wasn't the fortune teller on the way home? The noise of the street had grown to its early morning levels and she saw the teller's booth in the distance. A quick stop there and then to home she would go, barring any unforeseen events. She'd ask just a few questions and those answered, she would go from there. It would work out in the end. Tavera plodded through the streets, her thick boots keeping her feet stable on the slick streets, hoping a glimpse of what was to come would help her decide what to do before it came.

The fortune teller was easy to find. There were several of them in the town but the closest one happened to be the most trusted and was outside a store that sold lamp oil and lamps. The old woman sat directly under the sign bearing the image of an oil jar and a flame. The owner of the store was a thin man who supposedly owed part of his success to the woman and so she was allowed to keep her small operation located there, boasting an awning and an actual low table to display her fortune telling tools. The faded brown cloak that hid the old woman's form was meant to add mystery but Tavera was old enough and had been around enough fortunetellers to know better. She wouldn't fall for any act. However, it didn't mean this woman couldn't read signs pointing at what tomorrow held.

Tavera set two blueies on the low table and sat down on the ground before the woman, smiling as broadly as she could manage while tucking her legs under her. The time at the temple had cleared most of her hangover away but there was still a cloud in her head that she was hoping the fortuneteller could dispel. "I'd like to have my fortune told," she said simply.

The old woman looked up from her tools. Tavera saw bright red blood in one of her eyes and she tried not to react to the strange sight, though she felt the hair on the back of her neck stand up. Other than the strange eye, the woman was unremarkable. Her brown hair streaked with grey, the wrinkles around her eyes and mouth telling Tavera she was not old but not young, either. The woman's hands were steady as she gestured towards her tools, her eyes setting on her client. Tavera thought eventually the blood would pool in her eye and drip like a tear but it didn't. It just clung, bright red in the woman's grey-blue eyes. "What tools shall I use, what guide rings true for you, seeker?" the woman asked, her voice low but strong.

"Cards, please," Tavera said. The fortune teller removed the sticks, seedpods and stones from the table and picked the cards up in her long, skinny fingers. The cards looked to be new, shuffling crisply in her hands, the circles falling back into a pile. "And before you ask," Tavera offered, "I don't know what season I was born. I just want a reading for what lies ahead of me." The woman shuffled the cards one more time in a rather business-like manner, with an air of understanding.

Tavera knew some people had to be coaxed into believing with poems or little tricks, even after they had already paid. Some fortunetellers used such acts to hide the fact they had no skill in reading signs. But the girl knew sometimes the goddess could be reasoned with on the street corners more than in her own temples so she did business with the fortune tellers from time to time. This one was a professional. It made Tavera anxious to see what the cards held.

The cards shuffled, the fortune teller held them out towards Tavi and she gestured towards three, the woman pulling them out from the company of the others and setting them on the table. The woman then pulled out another three, setting them under the ones Tavi had picked before she pulled out one card to play the part of the goddess card, setting it over the others from where Tavera was sitting.

"The seen thing is the people come and work together for gain," the woman said, pointing to the cards. Each card did have at least one person on it, Tavera saw. Each deck of fortune cards was different from one another though the symbols were generally the same. All of the cards in the 'seen' row were waxing. Waxing had to do with gain, fruition and abundance. "However," the woman continued, pointing to the cards she had drawn. "The unseen thing is this. The secret blade comes in the night to cut the cord of love."

Tavera frowned. Love. She hated when that word came up in fortunes. The focus of the love itself could have been many different things, according to many tellers but this woman seemed more straight-forward. Tavera looked at the goddess card, the holy one's emotions regarding the reading and saw the waxing half moon. Tavera knew the card.

"Distress and hope," the woman said, pointing to the goddess card. "There is a lot of waxing energy in this pull, you should be careful not to get swept up into anything. You are bound to get in over your head." The fortune teller let Tavera look over the cards for a few breaths before she gathered them up again, shuffling them once before putting them back in their wooden box.

"Is that what the cards say, or what you say?" Tavera chided, seeing a smile form behind the woman's eyes. The woman pulled out her other tools and set them on the table for the next customer to choose from but not shooing Tavera away just yet.

"From me, of course," the fortune teller said, the bright red blood shining in her gaze. "I've been doing this a while. It's my input as someone who had been reading cards for a long time. Been doing it since I was younger than you." The woman looked her over and made a sound that was half a huff and half a laugh. "Though from the looks of you, you're very confident. You'll pull yourself up if you find yourself down, won't you?"

Tavera just smirked and brought her leg up, feeling the hard ground under her. She had another blueie in her pocket. What did she want to know about more? The group of people? The cord of love? The sword? Tavera pulled the coin out of her pocket and set it down on the table. "Could you tell me anything about this blade?" The blade was the most dangerous thing in the fortune and anything about it could identify the wielder. "Use whatever tool is best for that sort of thing."

Tavera watched as the woman pulled out a strip of cloth and a black stick, sketching the image of a sword onto it. She then pulled out a small vial of some liquid and dripped it onto the fabric, watching as the ink or chalk bled into the fabric. The fortune teller picked it up in her hands and squinted, the blood in her eye seeming to take up all the white as she did.

"The blade is not the sword of the Baron's seat. And it is an old blade. That is all I can tell." There was a bit of confusion on the fortune teller's face and the woman shrugged. Tavera was out of money anyway so she stood up and thanked the woman before she set off down the street back towards the inn. If anything started to keep her up at night, she would just have a go in the marketplace or try her hand at cards at the tavern and come back.

Well, the blade didn't belong to the sword and seat, that was good. It meant no one she knew would come under threat from the brown cloaks. And there hadn't been any mention of blood or death. Some fortune tellers liked to default to 'love' when she asked, falsely assuming that because she was a young woman, she was there to find out about a future husband or a lover. Tavera had been interested in shedding a bit of light on her situation with Lori but 'love' was a bit too heavy for that part to be about him. She liked him and maybe wanted to get some information from him. He was handsome and sweet. That was all there was to that. As for the rest of it, while it hadn't exactly cleared anything up it did give her a bit to look forward to. All the waxing cards meant growth and as for the secret blade, Tavera was good at finding out secrets. There was a chance she could find the unseen bit before its ominousness ruined anything. Her stomach growled and she remembered Derk's insistence upon her having breakfast and she smirked, knowing he had at least been right about that. Cruel about everything else but kind about that. Tavera laughed realizing she had just spent all her money at the fortune teller's, falling back upon the fact that she could just grab something on the way back towards their room.

Tavera walked, almost bumping into a young woman who was too busy ordering some men around to notice the thief, too engrossed in the task of pointing with a stick at the various items on a large cart. Tavera heard the young woman shriek as a trunk fell off the cart and spilled open, yards of fabric spilling onto the dirty ground. The man at fault shouted in protest as she raised the stick to hit him and people started to crowd and push, trying to see what the commotion was about. Tavera used the diversion to pull a bun off of a tray and she turned the corner and pulled it apart to see what it was stuffed with. Just honey and nuts. No phantom weapons whatsoever. She took a bite and tucked the rest away to give to Derk when she inevitably went back to the room. He would be hungry.

Chapter 9
A Cord, Cut

Tavera stopped dead in the street, suddenly remembering that she was in a different town and she was supposed to have turned left outside of the temple, gone down three streets before making a right and... she brought a hand to her head, rubbing her eye with the palm of her hand. Tired. She needed sleep. Now.

Praying hadn't helped her sort through the mess of action that had taken place within the last few days. Once again she ran through the chain of events leading up to her wandering the streets of yet another town...what was this one even called? A burp popped out of her mouth, remnants of last night's celebration, one she had been glad to be a part of but whose joy hadn't quite rubbed off on her. She found herself in front of the temple and ran over the directions once more before continuing on towards the inn.

The Dowry Take had ended well though bumps along the way had made it more nerve wracking than she would have liked. The goods were got and loaded as she herself had dictated but someone dropped a crossbow which discharged itself into the leg of the other thief. He screamed which brought attention and that is where the plan could have fallen apart. Tavera kept her cool and covered for the others as they escaped but had been found by the guard on duty who demanded that she give herself up for arrest.

Tavera hadn't planned for it to be Lori, she really hadn't. She knew his schedule and had chosen a day when she thought he would be off and miles away from the take. He must have switched watches. She didn't want to be taken in and he was going to do just that so she fought back and she sunk the point of her shortsword into his shoulder, pushing him back till his mouth opened with pain and surprise. She hadn't stuck around long enough to see if he would survive. All she remembered was running without sheathing her sword, getting to the wall and somehow getting over it. How she hadn't fallen on her own blade was beyond her. The party rushed with the cart for what seemed like forever, no light to guide their way save the stars. When they stopped, she jumped over the side and vomited in the bushes. Later as they rode away, she wondered if that was what the fortuneteller had meant. The old woman had said a secret blade would come in the night and cut the cord of love. She didn't love Lori. Did she?

Upon their arrival in Southpoint they divvied up the contents of the chest and found more than they had prayed for, much to their delight. The girl's dowry included many yards of beautiful fabric that could be sold quickly and fetch a good grip of money. There were spices and linens with easily removed monograms. Above the Inn they had divided the goods, Derk about to hand her her pile when he suddenly held back, a twinkle in his eye. He was smiling and the other men seemed pleased themselves as he spoke.

"Do you forfeit your share of the take as payment into the Cup of Cream?" he asked, his voice trembling with pride. Tavera had been dumbstruck. She had laid out the details of the Dowry Take, talked to the right people just enough, watching the home and help to get an idea of their movements; when she had mentioned the job to Derk all he said was, "Plan it out and let me know if you need anything. I'll see what I can do." She planned the take for the better part of the season, biding her time and patiently awaiting the day. It was only a fitting reason to leave the town with a good score. It turned out to be a test of her skill.

Her initiation took place in an abandoned building somewhere in town. Blindfolded and wet from the bath Derk gave her money for, she let them lead her to what sounded like a room underground. She was seated in a chair and given something unctuous and milky to drink, the warm liquid making her feel strangely alert. A torch was lit, the sound of it crackling crisp and clean and she heard people breathing around her in a circle.

"Who stands as witness to the initiate's worthiness to join our circle?" the voice said, its nearness startling her, making her jump in her seat. Her hands were bound and she was in her shift, the ropes starting to dig into her skin. Three voices rang out; one she recognized as Derk, one was Old Gam and the third may have been one of the fellows Derk rounded up for the take, possibly the one who had been shot. The rest of the circle was asked if anyone disputed her worth, to which no one replied. She was given another cup of something to drink, this one heavily spiced and sweet. Her blindfold was removed, her eyes adjusting quickly to the light, surprised at the number of people in the circle and even amused at some she found there, people she knew not to be thieves at all.

The person who had spoken first was a tall elf with black hair, his grey eyes narrowing at her as he took her hands, placing them on a set of thieves' tools, a pouch and a small painting of the moon goddess. Tavera swore to always practice the art of thievery, to carry herself as one who carried out the holy and ancient art form and to never betray her fellows, always watching for signs they were around her. She swore on the objects, one of the other attendees ringing a silver gong. Tavera was stripped of the name 'Kiffer' and given the name 'Point,' for her one intact ear and her blade that helped her fellows in what could have been a desperate situation.

Derk and she performed a ritual where their wrists were bound with a gold colored ribbon that was then cut, symbolizing that her apprenticeship was now over and that she now must answer for herself and to her fellows in the Cup. They taught her a handshake repeated with everyone in the circle and a slew of riddles and their answers were recited, each meant to be a sign post to others of the order so they might recognize her as one of their own. Someone sang the song of how the goddess stole light from her brother the sun, sanctifying the act of taking what wasn't rightfully your own. Then a communal cup was shared by the circle, this drink being sweet wine served from a decorated goblet, probably stolen before the order had been started.

After she was allowed to dress the initiation took on a more festive note. They moved things out of the building and into the bar below the room Derk was staying in. Tavera and Derk already hadn't been sharing a bed for a good spell but upon their arrival to this town Derk told his adopted daughter they could not stay together anymore since she was getting old enough to not be mistaken for his child and it was safer for both of them if they were apart. Any anxiety he had shown those first few days were drowned in ales and spirits, happy to see his daughter initiated. Tavera was ordered to drink anything they set in front of her and after a few drinks, unable to refuse anything set in front of her. Everyone laughed and drank, some sharing stories of trickster spirits, others telling graphic stories of exploits with members of the opposite or same gender, others told jokes or sang or danced. After a while it seemed like everyone was doing everything and Tavera blacked out while laughing heartily at a joke she thought she just heard. She dreamed fitfully of the young man she stabbed and an elven woman with long, black hair, her hands stretched out towards her but always keeping away.

She woke up in the bed of the elven man who had run the initiation. The only reason she knew this was because she recognized his clothing strewn across the floor, the tunic hanging halfway out the window. He wasn't in the room and she dressed and left the inn without running into him. If he saw her slip out, he hadn't called for her and she hadn't imagined he would have. It had been a relief.

That was why she had gone to the temple in the morning. To sober up and sort through her thoughts but the solemn atmosphere hadn't been enough to shake the girl clean. Tavera rubbed her eyes again, feeling the heaviness of them both, her head cloudy from deprivation and harried thoughts. Where the hems was she? Had she made a wrong turn again?

Her eyes widened as far as they would as she spotted a landmark she recognized. All she would have to do is turn left at the shoemaker's and....

Tavera kept on walking down the street though her eyes had seen what they had seen and her heart was telling her not to do what she was supposed to do. She walked down the street, past the inn where Derk was staying, counting the two guards that still stood outside the door, the innkeeper gesturing wildly and swearing at them. At the nearest alley she turned, heading down the narrow street, the dingy grey of the cobblestones and bricks blurring as she stumbled, keeling over and vomiting onto the ground.

They had Derk. She had walked by two guards who held his limp body between them, his head bowed and blood matting his hair to his head. He wasn't dead. If he was dead they would have called a cart; if he was dead, she would not have been able to keep it together. She had to keep it together. Is this why there had been a vein of nervousness throughout the week of festive yet furtive preparation? He almost pulled out of the take, she knew he was thinking about it but at the last minute said he was back in, adamantly so. Why had they taken him? What had he done? What did they say he had done?

She wiped her mouth with the back of her hand, stepping away from the puddle of mess left on someone's back doorstep. Tavera peered around the corner, looking towards the inn and then down the street. They had taken him from her. She wanted to go after them and get him back, rescue him. But Derk had made her promise in the temple, before the Goddess. Derk was alive but said if she wound up in the Jugs besides him, it would kill him. He told her time and time again she must be true to what she was, and what she was a thief. Tavi must strive to be the best she could be and part of that striving was to stay out of jail so she could continue to do what she did best. But Derk couldn't go to prison. He told her not to get caught. Maybe she could get him away from the guards before they put him in lock-up. How could she do it?

The Cup. Her feet were already flying back to where she thought she came from, not caring people were staring at her as she ran through the strange streets, her skirts fluttering behind her as she dodged between people and objects. A few wrong turns and some backtracking led her to the inn she had just come from and the stairs to the rooms. Tavera cursed as she tripped on the stairs, running up the rest on her hands and knees and throwing open the door to the room she had been in just a few hours before.

It was empty.

Empty. The bed was made, the window was closed, and the table and chair were in their proper place. Maybe she had the wrong room, she thought. But there was a crack in the mirror on the table that she vaguely recalled…had he left already?

As quickly but more carefully than before, she rushed down the stairs into the main area where the tender was waiting on a few early patrons. Her finger tips tapped the bar top rhythmically, her anxiety apparent as she tried to make eye contact with him. After what seemed like an eternity the tender came by, an older man with a scar that ran over where his right eye should have been. "What'll it be?"

"There was a Forester here, tall, older than me, grey eyes, dark hair. He's checked out, I believe but I need to know where he went." She hoped he would sense the urgency of her situation, prayed he knew the answer to her question. The old man shook his dark, sullen head, taking a bottle out from behind the bar and setting a glass in front of her.

"I ain't seen him this morn, but yer father was here, asking about ye. Ye best be on yer way now, miss, he's looking fer ye." He poured her a drink and went back about his business, leaving her there staring at her glass.

Milk. The guards were looking for her or at least asking about her. Tavera visited Derk enough times during the last few days. Someone must have placed them together and now the guards thought she knew something. Nervously she rubbed her wrists, anticipating the feeling of shackles around them, surprised to find the remnants of the gold ribbon, festively tied in a decorative bow by some other person last night. Her eyes watered as they fixed themselves on the frayed edges, ceremoniously cut by a simple dagger just last night.

They were looking for her and if the tender was in the Cup, she wouldn't endanger him by sticking around. She lifted the glass to her lips, gulping the milk down, careful not to swallow the coin he had been kind enough to drop into the bottom of it. She waved goodbye to the tender and left the bar, heading down the street that would get her to the eastern road the quickest.

Tavera wouldn't have to go back to her room. She had paid for the week and if she didn't show up by the end of the day the innkeeper would be glad for the extra income and rent it out to someone else. There was nothing left to fence and she carried a few changes of clothes and her tools on her, all she needed. Not all she needed, she thought, keeping her eyes focused on her feet as they carried her out of town. Tavera had been through what most children growing up in cities had. She'd been sold and beaten and sold again, overworked and underpaid, abused verbally, physically and mentally. Hunger, thirst and loneliness were things she knew all too well. Fear and pain had visited her often growing up. But she felt as if her heart were breaking, ripped out of her chest and carried farther and farther from her the closer she got to the edge of town. Long, thin fingers touched the golden ribbon around her wrist and she set her teeth against each other, forcing herself to walk away. She would leave the city and do what she was supposed to do, what Derk wanted her to do above all other things. Tavera would be Tavera, would be Point, would be what she was supposed to be. By herself and with the support of the Cup whenever she truly needed it. At least she'd have someone to brag to when she pulled something off. The thought of Derk's blue eyes not filling with pride almost made her cry and she felt like she was young again, alone with no one to love her anymore. Her arms crept up and she hugged herself as she pushed past people. Numbness trickled through her as she tried to brace herself against the emotions that wanted to well up again.

Why did everything have to happen at once, she thought to herself rather sardonically, managing a sad smirk as she fingered the frayed edge of the ribbon. First the take, the boy, the initiation and now this. What was next? The sun was a few fingers over the horizon, yellow now and calling to her as more of the city fell behind her. People, the wrong people, were probably looking for her and she didn't want to be here anymore. If she were to start fresh like Derk wanted her to, she would have to go somewhere else. Friends were easily made and connections established out of necessity. Family would have to be left behind. Fighting the urge to scream, cry or run, Tavera walked alone wondering what would come her way. She had her fill of bad luck. Someone owed her a bit of good and she was more than obliging to accept it.

Tavera was too good to just wind up in prison or cry herself away. As she wiped her tears the gold ribbon brushed against her cheek. She stepped past the gate towards the Freewild and the Eastern Valley, knowing she was more than capable to meet whatever came her way.

ABOUT THE AUTHOR

Tristan J Tarwater is the author of The Valley of Ten Crescents series. Born and raised in New York City she remembers reading a lot, visiting Museums and the Aquarium frequently and wanting to be a writer from a very early age. Her love of fantasy and sci-fi spills over into what she reads and watches in her free time as well as the collection of dice, books and small metal figurines that reside in her home.

Her work can also be found at Troll in the Corner (trollitc.com) where she writes the weekly column "Reality Makes the Best Fantasy".

She currently lives in Central California with her Admin, Small Boss, a cat that knows it's a multipass and Azrael.

http://www.backthatelfup.com

Other Works by
Tristan J. Tarwater

The Valley of Ten Crescents Series
Self-Made Scoundrel
Little Girl Lost

Other Stories
Botanica Blues

TRISTAN J. TARWATER

SELF-MADE SCOUNDREL

THE VALLEY OF TEN CRESCENTS BOOK TWO

LITTLE GIRL
LOST

A valley of ten crescents tale

TRISTAN J. TARWATER

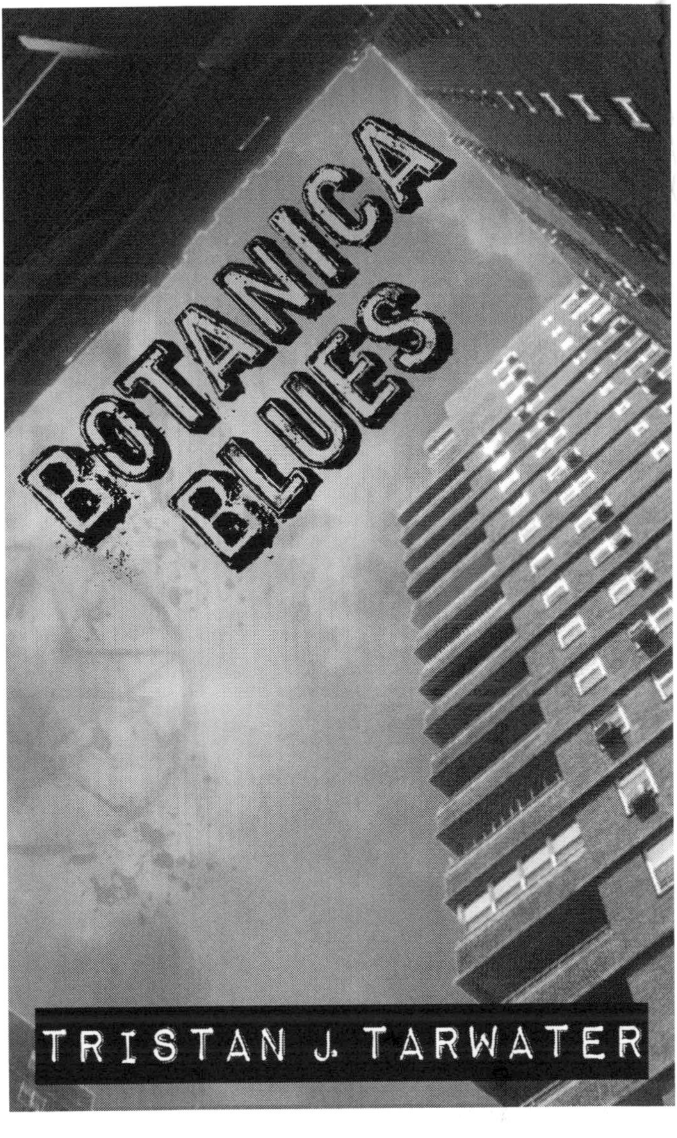
BOTANICA
BLUES
TRISTAN J. TARWATER

Made in the USA
Charleston, SC
24 July 2012